Reaction to MP Soldo's debut novel

ALEXANDRIA
THE STONES OF MACEDONIA

"A brilliant journey of tragedy and triumph where history and mystery engage you more with every page. Watch out for MP Soldo."
     - John Castagnini, Creator of ThankGodi.com

"…beautifully written…makes history a pleasure to read."
     - Robert Hecker, Author, playwright, former national president of Information Film Producers of America, Pasadena Playhouse 2012 Man of the Year, recipient of six Air Medals and the Distinguished Flying Cross

"…reveals an important era in mankind's development…. MP Soldo has written about a time where new ideas were triggering the advancement of the civilization of man. The time of Alexander the Great and his relationship with Ptolemy is an incredible one. Mr. Soldo has the one great gift every writer of history needs...amazing descriptive abilities. His words take you there...the sights, the sounds,..bring a virtual reality to the reader. Not only do you learn the facts, you are entertained by the unique style of writing. This is a fulfilling journey into the past. Read it. I'm sure you will agree."
     - Laura Manning, Lyricist, Member of ASCAP, Performer

This is a work of fiction. Details such as names, characters, or events were the creation of the author or used fictitiously. Any resemblance to actual persons, living or dead, is purely coincidental.

www.mpsoldo.com

This book is dedicated to my Uncle Jim for his bravery, dignity, and warm presence in our lives.

It is also dedicated to the fond memory of my two dogs lost this year, Toby and Jordan. Toby was a gentle Husky whose time with us ended far too soon, and Jordan was my best and most loyal friend for twelve years - a playful Lab that squeezed every ounce out of his long and glorious life. Jordan was always with me, and always my shadow, even as I wrote this book. From the first time I saw his eager face through a chain-link fence, to the last subtle wag of his weakened tail the morning he passed, he never failed to part my clouds, making my days forever shine.

"Shhhh, your grandfather is sleeping."

The little boy stopped running and slowly approached one cautious step at a time. As he peered over the tall bed surrounded by hanging fabrics, he could see his grandfather's large gray eyebrows dancing on an aged and scared face. He grimaced and winced, making painful muffled sounds. Then after a silent pause, the old man mournfully mumbled, "My love, I'm so sorry."

One of the guards standing outside the room glanced in to make sure everything was all right.

The boy then whispered, "Is something wrong with him Mommy?"

"Mmm no, he's just dreaming."

The boy then asked, "Are they *good* dreams?"

Chapter 1

Over two thousand three hundred years back into the ages, in the legendary land of Greece, Egypt, and Babylon, quests for power and conflicting ideologies erupted into violent campaigns across the known world. Clashing value systems of faith versus science and East versus West were settled by the sword. Yet, in all the bloodshed and brutality, humanity was on the verge of something wonderful - something that continues to challenge our infinite imagination, even until today.

It all began on one early morning of that ancient time, in a land to the north called Macedonia. There was a village, and at the far end was a busy pathway full of people hurrying about their day. Some carried loads of produce to sell in the village center, while others pushed carts or had animals in tow. Most wore light linen robes or dresses, with leather sandals.

Directly in the middle of this pathway, an elderly man separated from the moving masses and slowed his walk until he stopped.

At this very moment so long ago, a beautiful seed was about to be planted.

In one hand was a large stack of blank parchments clutched to his chest, and in the other a writing tool. Many people rudely bumped into the old man without a single request for pardon. As he turned, his aged but kind eyes tried to make contact with anybody in the crowd, but they were only met with downward stares and bothered looks.

And so right there, directly in the middle of this pathway, the old man closed his eyes, took a deep breath and kneeled to the ground.

At the other end of the village, a little boy woke from another one of his nightmares. Wiping his wet eyes he tried to clear his mind of the horrific vision that had pursued him night after night. It was a vision of agonizing and consuming fire.

The boy's family was influential in the community, and only employed the best intellectuals to school their son. But in the coming days, he would miss his scheduled sessions. After eating his breakfast, he walked outside his home, but something was odd. The sky had a strange, red glow.

At the pathway, undeterred by all the people, some almost falling over him, the old man set his stack of parchments down, opened the ink well and began to write.

Soon voices could be heard from the moving crowd. Some demanded he get out of the way, while others began to ask what he was doing. But as they passed, they heard no response from the old man.

He just continued to write.

One woman appeared and kneeled next to him. She placed her hand on his shoulder and asked if he needed help. He could feel the warmth of her touch and looked up into her eyes. She asked, "What are you writing there?"

The man quietly murmured, "*All that is.*"

The woman stood with concern on her face, but was pulled back into the moving crowd.

By the afternoon, many pages were now filled with writing, and a large crowd formed around the old man. Much discussion ensued, and all attempts to ask what he was doing were ignored. As time passed, some left the circle, but more joined, and so it grew.

By the evening, most of the village had now heard of the man at the pathway. People spoke of him at supper and debated what to do. Many went back, but by this time the circle had grown so much it was difficult to see. People stayed for many hours, but as the night air became cool, the crowd began to dissipate. By midnight everyone was gone.

All alone, in the light of the moon, the man continued writing.

And also alone, tucked away in his bed at the other end of the village, the little boy began to cry. His nightmare found him again, and for many long and painful hours, the boy's mind endured horrible torments of fire and great loss.

In the morning, people woke with the question of the old man on their mind. Is he still there? Why is he doing this? What is he writing? Many felt he was just crazy and surely had gone home by now. But curiosity was strong, so in the morning light, people rushed back to the pathway.

The crowd quickly became larger than it had the previous day, with hundreds now climbing the nearby grassy hill in order to see. Far from the back, a faint voice called out asking if he was still there. A man in front replied, "Yes, I can see him. He's still writing, and there's a dog with him now." Another person yelled out, "Maybe the dog is telling him what to write," and everyone laughed.

The old man never looked up once, and just continued to write.

As the day evolved, so did questions from the crowd. Some grew angry with the man and demanded he answer them. One woman yelled, "Why are you doing this to us?" Her overweight husband tried to read what was written, but as he approached, the dog quickly stood and showed his teeth. The woman's husband fell back on his rear, which resulted in more anger and commotion.

"We have to stop this," the woman yelled. Agitation grew and things were now being thrown at the man. A half-eaten apple bounced from his shoulder and hit the stack of writings. The old man severely weakened from lack of sleep and sustenance, stopped, put everything back in order, and continued writing.

As the late afternoon approached, the red glow in the sky became even more pronounced. The boy with the nightmares was one of the last from the village to join the crowd, which was now yelling and throwing more objects. He climbed a tree so that he could see.

But just as the boy looked, a large rock suddenly hit the old man directly on the head. He fell back as blood poured down his face. The boy couldn't take the sight and quickly covered his eyes. The dog stood over the old man, protecting him as he rolled and cried out in pain.

Cheers and laughter came from the crowd.

Slowly, the old man struggled to raise himself and wipe his blood-stained, teary eyes. His hands trembled as he picked up the large stack of parchments, now fully covered with his writings. He then began a methodical search through the hundreds of pages, pulling very select ones out of the stack. A voice yelled, "What are you looking for old man, your mind?" which again was followed by laughter and more yelling.

After going through all the parchments, the old man set aside seven in total, each marked with the blood from his hands. He then grunted in pain as he pushed himself up and slowly managed to stand. The crowd fell silent, waiting to see what he would do next.

Trembling with weakness, the old man sternly looked at the mass of people, studying each individual set of eyes. As he turned, he noticed the boy in the tree still shielding his own eyes from the terrible events.

The old man intently studied the boy while the crowd became more agitated than ever. With the large stack of writings in one hand, and the seven he separated in the other, he slowly began to walk towards the tree.

Someone said, "Where you going old man?" and pushed him from behind. He stumbled into another person who in turn shoved even harder, causing him to drop the large stack of writings. The old man looked back at the pages scattering in the wind and groaned, but remained undeterred. He regained his footing, clenched down on the remaining seven parchments that he selected earlier, and continued.

When the boy uncovered his face, he could see the old man was walking directly towards him with eyes locked on his. The crowd fell into complete chaos as they followed him. One man took the dog as another shook his fists with rage and yelled, "Stop him!" People continued violently pushing him from side to side, but he barely managed to stay on his feet.

Finally, at the base of the tree, with all his remaining energy the old man reached his quivering hands up to the boy and extended the seven pieces of parchment. The crowd became infuriated. One person stepped forward and punched him on the back of the neck. The boy quickly reached down and took the parchments before the old man collapsed to his knees.

In his very last moment, the man cried out to the boy, "Keep them safe. They are all that is good."

The crowd then closed in, and the old man was taken down with a relentless beating. When it was over, he lay motionless at the foot of the tree.

Still in shock over the entire event, the boy in the tree watched as people turned their attention from the old man, and began to fight over the parchments. Soon, everything was picked up and the crowds dissipated.

Later that evening, the people collected all the writings they could find and burned them in the village center.

But on that same night, in a large home at the far end of the village, the little boy placed the seven pieces of blood-stained parchments that he protected on the floor. He carefully arranged them in the candlelight and began to read.

In the coming years, the boy cared for them, studied them, and gained wisdom like no other in his village. He understood the significance of what the old man had done, and in time became a great leader, both loved and respected by his country.

When he would speak, he often recalled with painful sorrow the day the village killed the writing man. But then he would speak with sincere reverence of the *good things* that were so important, and how he protects them to this day.

Chapter 2

"Now, hold still or I'll pour this on your head!" A woman holding a vessel of wine was attempting to fill her husband's cup, but he was jokingly moving it back and forth. The woman sarcastically asked, "Do you want wine or not?" And with that, the man quickly stopped moving his cup and it was finally filled. The woman then sat in the chair across from him, and said, "Honestly, why do I put up with you?"

The man quickly replied, "Because no man can love you like me, and that's a fact."

"Yeah, well another fact is that no other woman can love you. And I mean that. Nobody! So you better be good to me old man."

The man chuckled to himself and took a drink.

After a moment, the woman looked around the room, and then quietly whispered, "He's been asking about you again."

Lagus groaned. "I'll talk to him, but mind you, I must always be hard on him, so he grows strong." The mother, knowing this was best, nodded her head in agreement.

After dinner, Lagus walked to his boy's room and peered inside. "You must have those memorized by now."

Startled, the boy looked up from his reading.

"Listen, I want to talk to you. Your mother said you were asking questions about me again." The boy sat up as the man continued. "She said you wanted to know if I love you, as I would my own son."

The boy lowered his eyes and nodded.

"Ptolemy, you know I must be strict with you. A Macedonian boy must not grow in comfort, but in struggle and challenge. That is not how you become just a man, but a leader of men, and because of that, my job is to be hard on you. But I'll forgo all that for the moment. Mind you, it is just for this moment."

"Yes sir."

"You're going to be nine soon, and old enough to understand many things. So I'll be direct. It's true your mother had another man in her life that fathered you, and some say it was the King himself. I can only assume this is what you have heard to make you question such things."

Ptolemy nodded.

"There are things we'll never know, and things we will. But listen carefully boy, for this is something you can know without question. My heart loves you as my son. You hear me? You will grow to be a strong man, and will achieve great things someday. Whatever people say makes no difference to me, and should make no difference to you. You're my son, and I'm your father, and that's our reality. You understand me?"

"Yes sir."

"Good. Now, there's one more thing I require before I leave."

Ptolemy's solemn face looked up.

"I need a smile."

The boy sat there with no response.

"Nowwww, I said I need a smile, and if I don't get one, do you know what I have to do?"

Ptolemy looked puzzled.

"I have to turn you upside down!" Lagus then hoisted Ptolemy over his shoulder. Laughter immediately broke out from the young boy as his father ran him into the main part of the house, but when Lagos saw Ptolemy's mother standing with hands on her hips, he immediately stopped and put the boy down. Lagus cleared his throat as Ptolemy ran out the front door.

"I see you're being extra hard on him!"

"Oh, you think you're funny do you?" Lagus then hoisted his wife over his shoulder and began to run her through the house as she screamed and laughed.

As Ptolemy grew under his parents love, so did his obsession with learning. He was intelligent and introspective, with great compassion in his heart. But in these brutal times, that quality was often mistaken for weakness, resulting in challenges and fights from other children. And this is why Ptolemy came to enjoy his studies and intellectual growth more than anything else. The more he learned, the more his thirst for knowledge grew, and the more his teachers had difficulty quenching it. However, the year finally came when Ptolemy's family could acquire a new teacher that was worthy of such a challenging task.

He was a wise and well-known man, educated by the great Plato himself. He had a full grey beard, flowing white hair, and the light in his eyes could ignite a forest during challenging dialogue.

After a few weeks, Ptolemy trusted his new teacher enough to finally ask for help with something that plagued him for quite some time. While in the garden where they had their lessons, Ptolemy told him the story of the writing man and the seven parchments he saved. As he spoke, his little forehead furrowed with tension. After Ptolemy finished, the teacher leaned back on the large rock he was sitting on, and asked, "Why would the writings of all these good things bother you so?"

Ptolemy shook his head. "No, it's not those. It's all the other parchments that were burned that night."

So with that cue, the teacher turned the conversation to the writings that were lost. "Why did he only give you seven parchments, and not all of them?"

Ptolemy narrowed his eyes and replied, "I don't know. I guess they were not as important to him. I think he just dropped them."

"And why do you think he didn't care about them?"

Ptolemy paused for a moment and said, "Since the seven he gave me were all that was good, he must not have cared about those things that were not good."

The teacher gazed into the sky, "Good Zeus, if he didn't care then why did he write them and give his life for them?"

Ptolemy paused even longer, and then said, "Maybe he had to write of the bad, in order to write of the good?"

"Ah!" The teacher's eyes lit up as he continued, "So the things that are bad, are connected to the things that are good?"

Ptolemy struggled but the teacher would not break the silence. He wanted his student to think through the equation.

Ptolemy said, "Well, sometimes good things can come from bad."

"Yes they can, and more often than not." The teacher stroked his beard and continued, "But is there truly such a thing as *good*, or such a thing as *bad*?"

Ptolemy's eyes frowned in confusion. The teacher then said, "From an enlightened perspective, they are one in the same. My boy, from now on, I want you to think in terms of cycles between your perceived good and your perceived bad. Seek to understand the beautiful relationship between the two, and how they both serve a deeper purpose. In doing so, I promise you will find wonderful insight, including your true self."

Realizing an example was in order, the teacher then asked, "Do you recall anything related between the good and the bad that was written?"

Ptolemy thought for a moment. "I don't know. So many parchments were burned that night."

"Now, think boy. Was there any connection? Anything at all?"

Ptolemy looked to the side, and then said, "My father once told me he was able to read one of the parchments before it was burned. It said something about a woman whose child was taken away because of her infidelity. She felt so bad she pulled her own hair from her scalp." Ptolemy then thought very intently until he realized a connection. "Oh! One of the parchments I saved is about family. It's one of my favorites. That's sort of connected, isn't it?"

"I would think so. And do you think he could have written with such passion about family, had he not considered the woman's agony in losing hers?"

"No teacher."

"Now tell me of the woman."

Ptolemy slowly responded, "Well, like you said, she was probably unhappy because of what she did, and having her child taken away."

"So how can she ever be at peace again?"

The young man looked his teacher in the eye and replied, "Maybe if she doesn't do it again? Perhaps if she thinks about the child she lost, maybe she would be a better mother next time? Maybe she could even be a better person?"

The teacher was so impressed he sat up in his seat and followed with another question, "And what if she doesn't associate the two?"

Ptolemy deeply considered this and replied, "Then her pain would be destined to repeat."

With that realization, the pleased teacher reached into his pocket. "I once visited a distant place called Magnesia, and was given these." In his hand were two oblong-shaped stones with a coppery finish. He handed one to Ptolemy and asked him what was so special about it.

Ptolemy examined the stone, and even licked it to see if there was a taste. "It's just a stone", he concluded. The teacher then put the second stone from Magnesia in Ptolemy's other hand.

Ptolemy quickly responded, "This is also just a stone."

"Is one better than the other?"

"No."

"Is one bad, and one good?"

Again, Ptolemy said, "No."

The teacher then instructed Ptolemy to place the stones together. The young man did this, and with a "click" they quickly flipped around and attached to each other. Ptolemy's head went back and his eyes opened wide. He pulled the stones apart several times to observe the magical and invisible force that drew them together, holding them tight.

The young Ptolemy slowly spoke. "Each stone is just a stone. But somehow they pull at each other, until they connect."

"Ha! And so it is with what we perceive as the good and the bad in our lives. The force behind this is invisible, but strong." Looking down at the stones, the teacher finished his point. "Separate, they are restless, continually attracting each other with consequences destined to repeat until one day the relationship of both is not only considered, but their purpose fully realized. Only then will the stones complement each other, fulfill each other, and only then will cycles end, bringing harmony and wisdom."

"But what of the bad things that are completely out of our control? Do they serve us too?"

"Well, the God's are indeed mischievous, and thus we will never understand all events that occur in our lives. But if you consider what I'm telling you, you will find that many times good and bad are related, and together as one is when they serve you best."

The teacher put both hands on Ptolemy's shoulders, "With this understanding...maybe now you can tell me why the village burned the writings?"

Ptolemy contemplated and then cautiously replied, "Because without considering the good things, they didn't understand how the bad actually helped them?"

The teacher gave a thunderous "Yes! And therefore, I must ask, can we always say that there is a difference between good and bad?"

Ptolemy's puzzled face finally brightened as a striking realization set in. "No...no we can't. Sometimes there is no difference at all!"

The teacher placed his hand on the back of Ptolemy's head, and gave a long, hearty laugh.

Chapter 3

Ptolemy loved his lessons in science and philosophy, but after several years with his wise teacher, time came to shift his education towards something of a more practical nature. As he sat at the dining table, Ptolemy's mother admired his wavy blond hair and thought to herself, "What a handsome young man", but his sad blue eyes looked up at her.

"Where's your smile my son?"

Ptolemy was usually content, but not today. He replied, "I need to ask my teacher more questions, and I'm not sure he'll be interested. It's not related to military tactics."

"It's those parchments again, isn't it?"

Ptolemy took a deep breath and nodded. She lifted his chin up, and said, "I have an idea. How about you give these to him?" She turned around and picked up a basket of grapes and a vessel of wine. "Bring these and maybe he'll be more willing to discuss the things you want."

Ptolemy's smile returned. As she watched her son running up the path, it reminded her of previous years, when he was a little boy, always curious, always on a mission of some sort. She yearned to hold him just one more time, and to gently rock him and sing to him, but resisted the temptation to even mention such a thing.

As his mother expected, Ptolemy's teacher permitted him to ask more questions about the writings. Sitting with his teacher in the garden, Ptolemy began to reflect, "It's still the same. I'm still bothered by all the writings that were burned that night." Ptolemy put his hand to his forehead, and then looked to his teacher for help.

The teacher grinned and said in a deep and warm voice, "I knew this has been your concern. Come boy, let's walk." The man leaned forward on his cane and stood from the large rock. Ptolemy also stood and walked by his teacher's side.

As they followed the pathway through the olive trees, the teacher looked at his student and asked, "So, you feel a great loss do you?"

Ptolemy nodded.

"And because of the writings that were burned, you feel disadvantaged, because you think knowledge was kept from you."

Ptolemy showed interest as the teacher continued, "I allowed you to bring this subject up again, because it has a direct application to our military lessons."

The teacher stroked his beard and asked, "Did you think about my proposition from last week?"

"Which one teacher?"

"My proposition that the things we do not know, tell us more than what we know."

Ptolemy put his head down and said, "Yes, but I still don't understand, because the things I don't know tell me nothing."

A long laugh rolled from the teacher's large belly. "Never forget young man, there is great value in understanding that which an opponent allows you to know, and that which he doesn't. By focusing on what is known, you become predictable. Seek to understand what you were not allowed to know, and there is your advantage." The teacher placed his hand on Ptolemy's shoulder. "There is much to learn about this, but not from me."

The two walked to the far end of the garden and down a winding trail leading to the beach. When the full glory of the Aegean Sea came into view, Ptolemy could see a small boat anchored thirty feet out from shore. There was a boy, years younger than Ptolemy, standing proudly on its deck. His blond hair was lofting in the wind and his piercing steel blue eyes were locked on Ptolemy's. He had a tall and strong posture, and his head was tilted slightly back so that his eyes had a downward angle. Despite his young age, he stood with such prominence it was clear this was somebody extraordinary.

Ptolemy and his teacher stood there, basking in the stunning image before them. The teacher said under his breath, "I want you to spend time with him."

A concerned expression grew on Ptolemy's face. "But he is so young. Is he your student?"

"No. But I suspect he will be someday."

"Then what can he possibly show me?"

The wise teacher chuckled and looked back towards the boat, "Oh you'll be surprised what you can learn from that one. Just think of what I told you, and you'll be fine."

With that reassurance, Ptolemy waded out in the water and climbed into the boat.

The teacher watched as the anchor was lifted and the boat silhouetted in the golden morning. From his perspective, it was being pulled out to sea not by wind, but by destiny.

In his long flowing robe, the teacher stroked his beard and contemplated the future of these two incredible spirits from Macedonia - one destined to be a conqueror, and the other a savior. And like the stones from Magnesia, he simply placed these two naturally opposing but complimentary forces together so that they may align.

Only this legendary intellectual, who carried the name of Aristotle, could understand the immensity of this moment.

<u>Chapter 4</u>

Seventy years later

If your ship were nothing but cedar planks and simple reeds strapped together by rope, sailing on the Aegean Sea would be a daunting venture, even with the gracious consent of Poseidon. But Demitri and his family accepted the risks, and sold everything they owned to enter the trading business.

Being their first passage, Demitri wanted to leave his wife and son behind, but Alena convinced him otherwise. So together, they bravely set out into the open sea, searching for a future of fortune and new experiences. On the third night of the crossing, Alena was at the bow of the ship when Demitri came from behind and spoke in her ear, "The cool air feels good tonight."

Alena leaned back into her husband's arms, placing her hands over his. The sea was gentle, but the dark of the night still intimidated her. "Our ship glides on the black water, yet the moon above doesn't move. And it is so big and bright, but darkness surrounds us. Oh my husband, what mysterious future awaits us?"

In the far distance, directly ahead of the boat, Demitri could see a pinpoint of light, stirring his imagination. "I think it's going to be amazing my love."

By the early morning, Demitri's navigator brought their ship safely to the coast of Egypt, at the most renowned shipping port in the ancient world.

The entire harbor was brimming with excitement as ships arrived, local venders sold their goods, and traders conducted their business. And exactly as they had heard, there was an enormous lighthouse towering on the edge of the harbor, looking out to sea.

After landing and securing their vessel, Demitri's crew quickly departed with wages in hand, while Demitri's young wife Alena endeavored to make herself more "presentable".

Once ready, Alena rushed her husband to the docks to peruse the exotic goods from around the world. This was their first experience away from the village in which they were born, and now they were standing at the foot of an exciting new future.

But the feeling changed in an instant. Just twenty minutes after arriving, their son came running. Out of breath he cried out, "Soldiers! They're on our ship!" Demitri took a deep swallow and his face turned pale. He looked to Alena and in a panicked voice said, "The gold!" As the family desperately ran up the dock, Demitri thought of all the valuables they left under the bench in their ship. It represented their entire life savings, and was needed to purchase goods, supplies, and a crew to return to their country. If taken, it would leave them stranded in a foreign land.

When they approached, two Egyptian soldiers stepped forward and stopped the family while three others conducted a methodical search of the ship. Alena began to say something but Demitri immediately shushed her. The boy stood behind his father and nervously watched as each container was opened and inspected.

The look of sheer agony was on Demitri's face as his family's dreams were disintegrating before his eyes. Then, just as he feared, Demitri could see a soldier, just inches from the bench that was hiding their gold. He leaned forward to intervene, and now it was Alena that shook her head to stop him.

Although the soldier already took another direction, Demitri's reaction caught his eye, so he turned back to the bench. He removed a blanket that was covering it, and noticed the top was slightly dislodged, exposing a hiding space underneath. He reached down and violently tore the lid off exposing the contents inside. Demitri lurched forward but he was instantly thrown to the ground and held with a foot to his throat. Alena screamed, but she too was restrained.

The soldier bent over and began to remove the contents. He pulled out a book in the form of a scroll that was gifted to Alena before they left, several other papyrus scrolls, some jar containers, and Elena's personal jewelry. Then, with a groan, he lifted a heavy wood box, but it slipped from his hands and smashed on the ship's floor. Hundreds of gold coins came spilling out. The soldier looked back towards Demitri with an odd grin on his face.

Demitri struggled and Alena cried out, but there was nothing they could do. Their life savings, and their only way home, was now in the hands of these soldiers.

But the horror of the moment was about to exponentially grow. Suddenly their son jumped towards the soldier with a knife in his hand. "Theo, NO!" Demitri yelled, but it was too late.

The boy's knife struck the soldier in the exposed part of his thigh. The soldier instinctively pulled the knife out and threw the boy to the ground holding the knife to his throat. Blood came pouring out from the soldier's leg.

Demitri and his wife desperately cried out, begging the soldier to take the gold and spare the boy, but the soldier couldn't understand their Greek. As they watched, he repositioned the bloody knife in his hand, and raised it above Theo's chest.

The boy closed his eyes, and so did Demitri and Alena, but the knife did not come as they expected.

The soldier instead tossed it from the boy's reach, and then ordered one of his men to assist him. The gold coins were gathered up and returned to their place in the bench, and the jewelry and jars were also returned. The soldier even picked the boy up and brushed him off, despite the large wound inflicted on his leg.

The soldiers then left, but they were not empty handed. The book and the other scrolls were taken.

Demitri couldn't understand why they left the gold, but that was not important at the moment. He and Alena hugged their son in relief, and all night Demitri stayed awake watching over his family. The next morning, although exhausted, they decided to refocus their energy back to the trading business at hand.

The days that followed were productive for Demitri. He made several contacts and conducted the business deals he needed. He was finishing a transaction with a local vendor and shaking hands when he noticed soldiers approaching his boat again. And like his worst nightmare come true, they went directly to his boy Theo. Demitri knew they came to punish him for stabbing the soldier. He screamed, "They're taking my son", and once again found himself running towards his ship in a complete panic.

But when he came closer he could see they were not taking the boy captive after all. Instead, one soldier, with a large bandage around his leg, was handing Theo a small but delicate object. All other soldiers then took turns patting Theo on the back, set some other items down and then left.

Once at the ship, Demitri looked at Alena with astonishment. In Theo's hands was a tiny model of their ship, carefully crafted by the soldier's son as a gift. And on the ground he saw the book and the scrolls previously taken. Demitri said in confusion, "I don't understand. They returned your book, and my inventory lists. Why would they do that?"

Alena then noticed something odd. Although it looked like the original book, it wasn't. Every single word, on every single page, was painstakingly copied by hand. "This is not mine, it's a copy." With a puzzled look, she asked, "Where's my book?"

The Great Library of Alexandria

Just a short distance away, an Egyptian worker was cataloging the very book that Alena wondered about. Once done, he proudly picked up the book and hurried down a serene path through a long and plush garden. The path, used only by the employees of the facility, ended at the foot of an enormous, man-made structure that had become the most prominent source of inspiration around the world: The Great Library of Alexandria. Scholars and philosophers without the means or the sponsorship could only dream of perusing its seemingly limitless collections, engaging in studies, and leaving their own legacy of works for all to use.

Stepping through the hidden doorway and into the grand entrance, the librarian paused to take in the stunning size of the building. He worked at the library for several weeks, yet was still lost in its enormity. Excitement filled the air as visitors were being escorted in all directions by staff, helping them find the various rooms or writings they were looking for.

After asking for directions from a more seasoned employee, the librarian proceeded up three flights of stairs and into a long hallway with beautiful mosaics below his feet, and colorful murals on the walls. Once he arrived at a particular conference room, the librarian paused to take a deep breath and straighten his uniform. He then quietly knocked on the door and opened it. Inside, six men in flowing white robes were engaged in a vigorous debate. With respect, the librarian placed the newly acquired book on the table and said, "This just came in, and may be of help." The six men stopped their arguing and looked with enthusiasm at the newly acquired parchments, bound together into a book.

At the dock, Demitri and Alena pondered everything that happened, but what they could not comprehend, was that the strange events of the last few days were set in motion over seventy years prior, when a simple but unlikely friendship started between two boys on a boat.

Chapter 5

With the lines of the sailing boat secured, Ptolemy sat back and watched his wise teacher fade in the distance as his new shipmate with a strong grip on the oar came into focus. At the same time, the salty air and the crisp sounds of the sea all became pronounced to his senses.

Ptolemy asked, "Is this your boat?" The boy quickly replied, "One of them."

"My name is Ptolemy."

The young boy remained focused on the sea and the ship's heading.

Ptolemy continued in a bragging tone, "Aristotle is my teacher."

Again, no response, so Ptolemy continued, "He told me to spend time with you, so that I may learn."

After a brief pause, the young boy exploded in laughter because he was told the same thing. But he didn't let Ptolemy know this.

Ptolemy jumped up and gave an odd look. Not understanding the humor, he asked, "What did I say?"

The boy replied while trying to quiet his laughter, "Nothing...everything."

Still not understanding, Ptolemy sat back in frustration, and then his eyes noticed the King's emblem on the boat's sail. He sharply asked, "How did you get this boat?"

More chuckling followed, but no reply to the question.

After following the coastline for an hour, the boat made progress, but the conversation suffered. Despite all attempts, Ptolemy didn't even know the boy's name, and so he was happy to see the shoreline finally approaching again. It was an expansive and complicated docking area with many ships unloading large cut stones and other building materials. "What is this place?" Ptolemy asked.

No response.

The small boat was slowly passing a much larger ship next to a dock, where two men were struggling to unload long, wooded beams.

"I order you tell me where we are!" Ptolemy said with a louder voice.

The boy stood and insolently replied, "Nobody orders me."

Ptolemy continued, "All I want is for you..." but his thought was interrupted mid-sentence when one of the large beams from the ship slipped from its straps and was heading directly for them.

"Get down!" Ptolemy yelled, but with arms folded and head tilted back, the boy started to say, "I kneel to nobody..." when the beam caught him square on the back, knocking him off the boat.

Ptolemy immediately began laughing as he watched a great commotion build in the water next to him. It was hard to tell, but the wild splashing seemed to be coming closer. Still laughing, Ptolemy peered over and in a mocking way asked, "What is that you're doing? Is...is that swimming?"

The splashing finally stopped as the boy reached the edge. A hand then slowly appeared, waiting for help. Ptolemy took the hand, but just before he pulled the boy up, he said, "First I want to know your name."

A voice from below finally conceded and said, "My...name...is", but then the boy gave a strong and sudden tug sending Ptolemy sailing over the rail. And just before he plunged into the cool Aegean Sea, Ptolemy heard for the first time this simple yet momentous name that would reverberate in his mind for the rest of his life: "ALEXANDER!"

Chapter 6

From the time they shared their first laughter, through all the military training, tutoring, and childhood adventures, Alexander and Ptolemy became close friends with a deep spiritual connection. But as time passed, Ptolemy could see restlessness growing within his friend.

Often Alexander would talk of a special connection with the Gods, and an unearthly destiny he would someday fulfill. While most rejected such comments as childhood fantasy, Ptolemy soon became a believer. And oddly enough, the events that led to his realization began just thirty miles to the East, at a well-established horse-trading business owned by a short and extra-round man named Philo.

The interesting thing about Philo is that despite his very profitable horse-trading business, he was lousy with horses. He was scared of them. He knew it, and unfortunately the horses knew it. But this didn't matter, because like all good businessmen know, you don't have to be smart and talented to be successful, you just need smart and talented people working for you. And in Philo's case, he had an excellent crew.

So when his latest acquisition arrived, he never imagined the trouble it would bring. The extraordinarily large horse had a black coat with a white star on his massive forehead. Although admired by the staff, they were greatly intimidated as they tried to tame it. Within three days all of his horse trainers were carried off with broken bones and smashed jaws.

To recover his losses, Philo was forced to send word to a distant competitor, where many believed two brothers had developed a method guaranteed to break the spirit of any horse. So at great personal cost to Philo, the two men finally arrived with equipment in hand to tame this now renowned horse.

Philo, holding a bag of gold coins, asked the men, "Are you really as good as everyone tells me?"

The younger brother answered, "No. Better."

The older brother grinned, and then said, "Our fee is six talents, nonrefundable, and payable up front. If he lives, he will be tamed."

Once payment was received, the two men began to gear-up. They slowly donned their outfits and weapons like warriors, and proudly waved to the crowd that has now gathered. After bravely entering the enclosure, both men maneuvered themselves on either side of the mammoth horse.

The horse quickly became agitated, so the lead trainer said, "Stop. Let me distract him first, and then you come from behind." He then addressed the horse now facing him. "Oh you're a big one. I think you want out of this cage don't you?" The horse snorted and flung his massive head up and down. "Oooo, a little angry too. We'll see how angry you are after this." He then shouted "Now!", and the trainer's brother quickly came up on the horse's blind spot and with a loud crack, clubbed the poor animal on the side of his head.

The horse grunted in pain and flung his head to the side. He lifted his powerful legs in defiance, and slammed them to the ground with a thunderous clap. Now his eyes were filled with rage, and his enormous muscles were fully tensed, ready to explode. The lead trainer gripped his club and closed in.

Philo, watching from a safe distance, turned to the man next to him and said, "I want you to watch this closely. These men are experts, and it's time our people learn how to do this right."

They both turned back just in time to see one trainer launching off his feet from a kick, and the other already unconscious twenty feet away.

Philo took a deep breath and in a defeated tone, said, "Get'em out of there."

Word soon spread of this magnificent horse that couldn't be tamed. So when Philo brought his stable to the King of Macedonia, he didn't expect the wild horse to sell. In fact, after hearing of the horse, King Philip turned the opportunity down.

As Philo negotiated with the King, the two boys were listening intently. Alexander leaned towards his friend and whispered, "I could tame it."

"No!" objected Ptolemy, but Alexander was already interrupting his father.

"I want the black horse."

King Philip laughed and said, "Boy, the price is thirteen talents, and he is far too much horse for you - too much for anybody."

Alexander then proceeded to present his case. Ptolemy watched with amazement as the infectious passion of the ten year old spread among the group. Even King Philip, who wasn't known for outwardly showing love or respect for his son, was amused by the offer and an agreement was made. If Alexander could tame the horse, King Philip would buy it for him. If not, then Alexander would pay for it.

Ptolemy tried to remind Alexander he didn't have thirteen talents, but Alexander quietly said, "I know." He then picked up the harness and carefully entered the enclosure. The horse looked like a mythological monster compared to the young boy. But within a few minutes, Alexander slowly positioned himself between the horse and the blinding sun.

"Very clever", Ptolemy thought. Alexander's voice soothed the horse as he approached, and by facing the sun, there were no shadows to startle it. At the slightest indication of stress, Alexander turned his face away to remove the threat, but continued his soft and melodic words, almost singing to the horse.

Ptolemy was amazed with his friend's patience, but as the hour passed, everyone had turned their attention elsewhere. Most of the men were still in the area, in deep discussion with their King. Everyone assumed that since it was quiet, that everything was at least progressing well.

But then suddenly a loud shriek came from the enclosure. King Philip instantly realized that allowing his son near such a large and dangerous animal was a grave mistake. The men quickly turned and began running as fast as they could. Ptolemy was nearest, but just as he approached the corral he was blasted with the energy of the powerful horse as it came bounding over the wall. From the ground where he was thrown, Ptolemy looked up to see Alexander was on its back, tightly holding on.

King Philip laughed with delight in seeing his son flying across the open plain on such a powerful and beautiful animal. He accomplished what grown men and so-called experts could not, and this made the King of Macedonia cheer as he never had before.

Later that evening, King Philip ate and drank excessively at a large banquet, and this time the boys were allowed to attend. Although his gregarious mood filled the room, everyone present knew it could turn bad in an instant. And that instant came when a voice from the room was heard above all others. "Look at Alexander over there, the horse tamer."

Another voice added, "Indeed, he can harness a horse, but can he ever harness a country?"

Alexander looked directly at the men verbally attacking him, but did not reply or even blink. Ptolemy, while also locking his eyes on the men, leaned towards Alexander and asked out of the side of his mouth, "Do you know these men?" Alexander whispered, "Admetos and Lampos. They're going to regret this."

King Philip did not defend his son, but instead added to the attack. "Answer boy! Will you be able to harness a country someday?"

Alexander did not want to engage his father while he was in such an inebriated state, and thus held his tongue. But soon the non-response began to anger

King Philip, so Ptolemy inserted himself by saying, "My King, only in the foot steps of a great father could a boy dream of such a feat."

With that statement, King Philip drunkenly swung his attention to Ptolemy. Interjecting between the King and his son could easily result in death, and now Ptolemy's fate was teetering and could fall on either side. Sensing his friend's danger, Alexander needed to bring the attention back to him. In a low voice, he said, "I only harness that which no other man truly can."

The room fell silent as King Philip turned his red eyes back to his son. The statement could easily be taken as a commentary on the King himself. Ptolemy wanted to intervene again for his friend, but he could not. Everyone held their breath. The King took another drink of wine and quietly chuckled, "Of that I do not doubt." The room relaxed and conversations and laughter slowly started again.

It was clear that Alexander annoyed some in the room, including his father. But there was a level of respect that was growing.

Later that evening, Ptolemy could see King Philip confiding in his son. The room was loud, so Ptolemy casually maneuvered himself just in time to hear Alexander say, "But I will be King, I can feel it."

King Philip looked down and replied, "Indeed my son, but seek a kingdom that's worthy, for Macedonia is too little for thee."

Ptolemy was quite pleased with the King's confidence in Alexander, but he was still leery of others in the court. And just over a year later, it became apparent that Ptolemy's instincts were correct.

Late one night, just hours before sunrise, Ptolemy was walking outside the palace gates along the dark path towards his home. He stepped over a fallen branch when movement ahead caught his eye. The moonless night made it difficult to distinguish bushes and trees swaying in the breeze from anything else. But his spine chilled and his breath went short. Something was wrong.

Ptolemy stopped but didn't see anything. Then sounds from behind made him look back, and through the darkness a figure emerged about twenty feet away. Turning to the front again he could see someone else the same distance ahead. Still not sure of the situation, Ptolemy discreetly reached for his small dagger, but it was not with him.

The man in front started calling out to Ptolemy in a strangely familiar voice, "Well look at the horse trainer's friend, all by himself, in the middle of the night." The man in back laughed as they both continued walking closer. "It's a shame you weren't home. But don't worry, your mother kept us entertained."

Ptolemy's mind spun as he tried to stem his anger enough to calculate an escape, but this part of the path was well chosen. There are only a few layers of trees before a rough terrain rising up steep hills on either side.

The two men were only ten feet away when Ptolemy leapt from the path and began darting through the trees at top speed. But just as the sound of the pursuing men began to distance, Ptolemy's leading foot smashed into a large rock sending him flying. Two of his toes were shattered and his face and hands bloodied from being grated across the ground. Despite the pain he quickly attempted to stand when one of the men landed directly on his back, slamming Ptolemy down again, knocking the wind from his lungs. The second man dropped his knees on Ptolemy's neck and head, shoving his face back into the dirt.

The two men kept all their weight on Ptolemy as they caught their breath. One forced Ptolemy's head up by his hair and bitterly ordered, "Tell that little friend of yours he better start to use his ears and listen to us, or what happened to your mother will happen to his."

The other man added, "And what's about to happen to you, will happen to him. You give him this message!"

And with that, one man pulled a knife from his sheaf as the other rolled Ptolemy to his side. The man with the knife wrapped his legs around Ptolemy to help hold him. Ptolemy struggled but it was of no use. The cool blade pressed against the base of his ear.

In this moment, time slowed as Ptolemy's mind became more observer than participant. He thought how odd that his ear was actually going to be sliced off, and then felt concern over his mother, and what must have happened to her. The sound of his own breathing became louder, and soon Ptolemy could hear his own heartbeat. The man's breath smelled of wine, and his warm perspiration began falling on Ptolemy's face. The drips became heavier, and thicker, running down the side of

Ptolemy's neck. Everything felt numb as he began losing consciousness.

But when the man's legs went limp and his knife dropped, Ptolemy returned back to the moment. The perspiration dropping on Ptolemy's face was actually blood, and it was not his. The man who was attempting to remove Ptolemy's ear fell backward making a loud gurgling sound from his neck.

Ptolemy then looked up to see the silhouette of a small man violently stabbing his other attacker in the neck and shoulders. The desperate cries and arms raised in defense were of no use. The man finally slumped back as the small figure straddled him, and used both hands to push the knife deep into his chest.

Ptolemy wiped his eyes so they could finally focus. It was Alexander, still sitting on the man's belly, staring at his very first kill.

With blood now dripping from his face and hands, Alexander climbed to his feet and walked to the other man whose windpipe he severed just moments prior. Again, using both hands and his full body weight, he forced his knife deep into that man's chest as well.

At just ten years of age, Alexander saved Ptolemy by killing two men. Despite all the blood and death around him, Alexander casually walked back to Ptolemy and peered down at him, making his wavy hair enclose his face. He then said in his youthful voice, "See, I told you."

Ptolemy mumbled, "Told me what?"

"I told you they would regret their words."

Chapter 7

Ptolemy often thought about the night Alexander saved him, but during the six years that followed he never spoke nor wrote one word of it. As far as the rest of the world knew, the two men that verbally challenged Alexander, and eventually attacked Ptolemy, simply disappeared.

One morning while leaving his home, Ptolemy directed his eyes towards the grassy rolling hills just outside his home where a man was running towards him from a far distance. When he finally arrived, the messenger dropped to one knee and took several large breaths before speaking. The urgent news he brought didn't surprise Ptolemy as he knew this day was coming.

When King Philip gathered his army and invaded Thrace, he left Alexander in charge as his regent. This meant for the first time, Alexander was effectively the ruler of all Macedonia, and bearing the entire burden of his country at just sixteen years of age. And unfortunately, it wasn't long before a hostile dilemma presented itself.

At the palace, Alexander was seated with three high-ranking soldiers standing in front of him. One disclosed the grave situation. "Scouts detected a large Thracian contingency building in Maedi." Alexander gritted his teeth and asked, "How many?" One responded, "It was night. They couldn't see individuals but counted over five hundred campfires. We estimate five to ten thousand men and growing." Alexander looked to the other two for input. One said, "Our reserve force is not enough. We must call at least half of King Philip's army back to defend us". The other said "No! Dividing the army would mean defeat in Thrace. We should wait and do nothing until they provoke us." The first man yelled, "Absolutely not! The more we wait, the more our enemy's forces build. We must call the King back now!"

They needed a decision, but Alexander only looked to the distance. He then said to the three men, "Leave me now." The men glanced at each other with concern and left.

Then, from the back of the room a friendly voice said, "I hear they'll make anyone ruler around here." Ptolemy stepped forward into the light. Alexander jumped from his chair and ran to his friend and embraced him. Ptolemy put both hands on Alexander's shoulders, looked into his eyes and said, "I just heard the King assigned you his ruling power." He then gave a long and thoughtful pause. "Are you ready for this Alex?"

Alexander almost didn't understand the question. This is what defined Alexander, and why he was put on Earth. There are no choices and no questions about it. He simply grinned and said, "Yes," and then continued with the issue at hand. "They want my father's main army to return and protect us, but I know that's exactly what the Thracians want."

Ptolemy paused and said, "But you can't ignore our enemy's force building on our border."

Alexander slowly nodded. "I know."

The next day Ptolemy watched as Alexander assembled the small reserve army of just under a thousand men. When there was a choice of doing nothing or sending for his father's return, he created a third option. And this option wasn't even presented to him by the experienced military advisors, which made it something the Thracians would likewise not expect. Alexander would confront the enemy uprising himself, in their own territory.

As Ptolemy continued to observe Alexander from a distance, a senior member of the ruling council standing next to him started talking in a snake-like whisper. "What a brave little boy. But that child doesn't know what he's doing. He doesn't have enough men to squash the uprising, and they will surely be killed." He then came closer to Ptolemy's ear. "If only there was someone close to him with influence. Perhaps we could convince him..."

Ptolemy sharply interrupted, "Watch your tongue! That CHILD is more MAN than you will ever be, so keep your cowardly comments to yourself or I'll rip them from your throat!" Even Ptolemy was startled by his own assertive response, something he learned from Alexander. The old man quickly withdrew and disappeared.

Once the reserve troops were ready, Alexander climbed confidently on the back of his large black horse and led the group in the direction of Maedi. Ptolemy was overwhelmed by his young friend's courage and the way he organized supplies and motivated the group so quickly.

Although gone from sight, Alexander was on everyone's minds. They thought of him, and honored his bravery.

After many weeks had passed, another messenger approached Ptolemy and just as before, he was not surprised by the news except that it came so soon. Alexander successfully squashed the uprising and was returning home.

This was a pivotal event for Alexander. Despite his young age, his initial encounter with the Thracians gave the soldiers a strong and lasting respect for him. Ptolemy asked the messenger for details.

"It was just as he promised us. The enemy numbers were far less than predicted. We have no idea how he knew." The man, bearing a fresh wound to the face looked down and continued with admiration in his voice. "His tactics were unpredictable, confusing, but worked without fail. And he fought side by side with us, with more bravery and strength than we have ever seen. I was there, and saw him. There was no fear in his eyes."

Ptolemy asked the man to rise and said, "You served Macedonia well soldier."

The man looked at him and replied, "Yes, we served Macedonia. We fought for her and our families. But we fought harder for Alexander."

Alexander's success became the topic across all Macedonia. And when King Philip received the news during his campaign in Thrace, he too was pleased.

Everyone was intoxicated with the wonderment of this sixteen year old, but there was something Ptolemy was curious about. So one day after Alexander's return, while walking together Ptolemy asked, "How did you know the Thracian numbers were less than estimated?"

Alexander began to talk around the subject when Ptolemy interrupted, "Alex, please tell me."

Alexander said, "Remember what Aristotle use to tell us? To focus on what your enemy doesn't let you know?"

Ptolemy thought for a moment until he came to a realization. "We never saw the soldiers, only camp fires!"

Alexander nodded and produced a devious grin.

Chapter 8

Ptolemy, now age thirty-one, is not just a friend, but also an advisor to Alexander. The years have placed a classic Greek profile to Ptolemy's appearance, and wisdom to his persona. His wavy, dark blond hair was long, but his face was beardless. Time has taught him that contemplation and careful analysis are rewarded with wise decisions. But it was Alexander, a true warrior, who taught him fearless and decisive action is rewarded with conquest and power.

Only two years have passed since King Philip's death, yet Ptolemy could sense that Alexander, now in his twenties, was no longer content with the throne of his country. His friend, and King, was on the verge of pursuing the very thing his father recommended: a kingdom worthy, which meant far more than just Macedonia.

Ptolemy also knew that Alexander's thirst for power would not only dominate his life, but the hundreds of thousands under his rule, impacting millions of people across the planet. It was too great of an imbalanced force, and Ptolemy foresaw horrors beyond imagination if left unchecked.

Knowing this was the right time, Ptolemy decided to tell Alexander about his closely guarded treasure. In a quiet room, he spread out the seven parchments he protected since childhood, and told the story of the writing man.

Alexander loved reading, and was intrigued. He began to ask questions about the parchments themselves, and what they were about.

"I believe each one represents a major facet of life that people value most. This one talks of all the good things that bring people closer to their own spirit, and to the Gods that created them. And this one of all the good that pertains to family." Ptolemy then began to scan over the others. "Health of the body, health of the mind, financials, one's trade, and one's friends and other relationships. They also speak of the precious liberty that people need to pursue these things." Ptolemy paused, and then looked Alexander in the eyes. "These must never be forgotten. Protect them Alex, and the people of your empire will grow to undreamed potentials."

Alexander was deeply touched by Ptolemy's sincerity, and read through several entries and asked more questions. He proudly accepted the parchments, promising to protect and honor them, just as the parchments themselves honored all that is good.

Ptolemy thanked his friend, and then asked, "What is going to happen next?"

"My Kingdom lies to the East – we just have to take it."

"Persia?"

"Yes, and beyond."

Ptolemy was already aware of Alexander's plans, but wanted to hear it directly from him. "Then what, Alex, when will it end?"

"When there's no more war, and just one rule." Alexander put his hand on the back of Ptolemy's neck and added, "It ends when all people have the freedom to pursue what's written on these parchments. And instead of the end, that will truly be the beginning."

Alexander then took the writings back to the palace and placed them on a table. He walked back and forth a few times while looking at them, and then called to his assistant. "Gather my men."

After a few moments, seven were standing in front of Alexander as ordered. "Each of you holds the most sacred position in my force. Not just personal guards, but commanders. You are my most trusted, and with that honor is a great burden each of you must bear." Alexander handed each one a parchment. "In the coming years, we will endure hardship and violence like never before experienced. You have three equal priorities: Protect these writings, protect me, and kill our enemies. Nothing else is more important, not even your own lives."

One of the seven stepped forward and kneeled. "My King, where will we be going?"

Alexander motioned for the man to rise and said, "Where few have dared to dream."

Chapter 9

Twenty-three days after Alexander's powerful legion started their great march to the East, Alexander took a small contingency on a detour to an ancient and sacred place called Abydos, in the land of Troy. At first sight it appeared to be just another desert plain, but here, on these sanctified grounds, famous heroes once stood. With a select number of his military leaders and his personal guards all standing behind him, Alexander removed his helmet and knelt.

The men closest could hear him murmuring, but couldn't make out the words. He chuckled to himself and then finally stood and turned to address his men. Behind him were faint remnants of a city, surrounded by thousands of ancient cut stones, lying in complete disarray and overgrown by thick grass and bushes.

Alexander's expression was sincere and focused as he slowly began to speak. "Diomedes, Philoctetes, Odysseus." Alexander extended a handful of dirt and let it sift through his fingers. "Eight hundred years ago, they stood on this very ground. Patroklos, and the greatest of them all, Achilles. Not just soldiers, but warriors."

Looking over his shoulder, Alexander continued, "These were impenetrable walls of stone, and behind them, the legendary Trojan army, impossible to defeat.

Yet look around, what do you see now? Are there giant walls? Is there a great city?"

The men looked, but only saw ruins.

In Alexander's mind, he saw a completely different scene. It was a green field where a young boy was walking with his teacher. The teacher was telling him the story of Troy and the heroes that fought there. It was a distant memory, but it came to him in an instant. The boy looked up and asked, "How did they do it? How did they defeat the Trojans teacher?"

Aristotle chuckled and replied, "They were warriors my boy. Warriors confront all fears and obstacles, and they never quit. Nothing, not walls, not armies, and not even time can stop them."

With that memory in mind, Alexander opened his eyes and engaged his men again. "For nine years Troy didn't fall. But in the tenth year, the Greek's were victorious." Alexander now began walking among his men. "Indeed, we too, will face glorious battles here in the East. But fortunate are we, for beating within our hearts are the hearts of thousands of warriors that came before us. Hear them now! Their battle cries echo in the valley. Their blood running in your veins, and their bravery in your hearts! Your fathers are calling you to join them in battle!" Alexander stood tall and raised his sword. Using all the air in his lungs, he bellowed out, "WILL YOU ANSWER THEM?"

Now energized, every man yelled, "YES!"

"AND WILL YOU FIGHT FOR THEM?"

"YES!!!!"

The energy flowed through every man, making it impossible to stand still. As they stabbed their swords to the sky and continued shouting, Alexander turned to his second in command, Parmenio, and said, "Prepare the animal sacrifices. It's time we bow our heads to Athena."

"And what of tonight my King?"

While watching the men rejoice, Alexander said, "Tonight we commemorate our honored Achilles. In his name we will prepare our bodies with olive oil. We will have competitions, and we will race!"

Chapter 10

A few days after paying homage to ancient Troy and the Greek heroes buried there, Alexander and his men rejoined their legion as they traveled deeper into Persian territory.

Every Macedonian knew that each step into their enemy's land brought them one step closer to the horror of battle: war cries muffled by sliced throats, broken bones piercing through torn flesh, trampled men suffocating in the mud, dismembered limbs and heads, and a ground no longer visible from all the lifeless bodies.

The absolute brutality made a quick death an almost welcome haven. Yet the men still marched on until the eighth day, when scouts returned with news of a Persian force positioned to intervene.

Alexander's army had now approached the Granicus River and the stage of conflict was set. Alexander surveyed the situation and devised a strategy. All around were open plains, with an enormous Persian force just a few hundred yards away on the other side of the shallow river. And like an enormous dark living organism, thousands of Persian soldiers were organizing and facing the West.

Parmenio approached and said, "My King, their numbers match ours."

Alexander did not respond.

Parmenio continued, "It's late. Best the men set camp and attack at first light tomorrow."

Alexander looked behind him towards the bright sun and then back to the Persians on the other side of the river. He called out to his troops, "Center Phalanx, hold!" Twice the Generals echoed his command. Turning back to Parmenio he said, "The sun would not agree with your advice."

Across the river stood thirty thousand of the mighty Persian force preparing to stop Alexander's invasion to the East. Some stood in brave but ignorant defiance, while others stood in concealed fear. Some hoped it would be their sword that claims the glorious honor of killing the Macedonian King, while others only hoped to see their loved ones again. Most were Persian born, and some were Greek, fighting as mercenaries. But no matter whom they were or what their motivation was, every single man stood that day with one thing in common: they all faced a blinding sun, thanks to the brilliant strategy of Alexander.

In the next tense but silent moment, a combined sixty thousand men from both sides of the river waited for this young Macedonian to take the most audacious step in history. With a single order, Alexander began what would be a series of brutal wars, which would immortalize him and change the landscape of humanity forever.

Macedonia

Three hundred miles away in Macedonia, Ptolemy was in a peaceful vineyard in deep thought. A warm voice from behind interrupted the solitude. "Have a moment for an old friend?" Ptolemy quickly turned to see the comforting face of Aristotle.

"Hello my boy, I've missed you. What brings you here by yourself?"

"I was thinking about Alexander."

Aristotle replied, "You look tired. I have always found deep contemplation to have such an effect."

"Alexander is across the Aegean, fighting the Persians. And I should be with him."

"I agree, so why aren't you?"

"I've already been banished once before for misadvising him."

Aristotle quickly interrupted, "At King Philip's orders, not Alexander's."

Aristotle paused, stroked his beard and then continued, "I heard news of what he did in Tyre. They say he destroyed it. He killed the men, and sold the women and children. You know Alexander won't stop there. His quest for power will continue, with brutality beyond measure. He needs the balance you bring more now than ever."

Ptolemy gazed at the blue sky, trying to picture what is happening at that very moment, in that distant land of Troy.

Granicus River

Alexander's first order of attack was issued to the infantry unit to his left. With strict military training since childhood, the men immediately reacted without question. As they charged across the shallow river on foot, the Persians heavily reinforced their right flanks with men and weapons and steadied themselves for the crunch.

Battle cries and the collision of muscle against muscle, and armor against spears echoed through the plains as the Macedonians slammed into the Persian lines. Some were pierced and fell, while others slipped and were trampled in the mud. Although brutal, this initial Macedonian attack was really just a distraction.

By reinforcing their right flank, the Persian center was now vulnerable, which was exactly what Alexander wanted. He pulled the reins on his horse making the great beast rear back on its hind legs, and then shouted, "Attack!"

A force of men on horseback quickly separated from the Macedonian lines and began tearing across the river with their young King in front.

Thinking they were successful in pushing back the first wave of Macedonians, the Persians were surprised to see a second wave rushing at them so quickly.

Two of the Persian soldiers standing in the front line looked at each other and swallowed. They were both from the same village and were close friends since childhood. They vowed to protect each other in battle so they could once again return to their homes.

As the Macedonians approached, a wedge was formed off each side of Alexander. The thunderous sound of their horses and their battle cries were bone shattering.

The two Persians raised their spears as Alexander's powerful black horse began large strides up the muddy embankment. One of the Persian's aimed a spear at the horse's chest but it didn't penetrate. It was deflected by armor as the large front hoof of the horse slammed into the Persian's chest throwing him off his feet. From the ground, he looked up to see his friend rushing the animal with his dagger, but Alexander's sword came slamming down across his back, leaving a large open gash. The severely wounded Persian covered in blood fell to his knees. When his friend called to him, the Persian had just started to turn when the horse's back hoof landed on his head smashing it instantly into the mud.

Alexander's eyes were locked open in a hyper-focused state. His enormous horse continued to plow fearlessly into the masses as men were relentlessly struck with his sword.

But Alexander was not left untouched. The first Persian that witnessed the death of his friend regained his footing and rushed Alexander from the side, slamming him on the head with a wooden club. Although he wore a helmet, the blow stunned Alexander. He would have fallen had it not been for one of his personal guards catching his body and holding him tightly on his horse.

After the Macedonian force pulled back to their side of the river, the Persians were left with a clear opening in their ranks that Alexander once again capitalized on. Despite the pain and vertigo caused from his head wound, Alexander yelled out, "Cavalry!"

With that order the full force of three thousand men on horseback raced across the water at top speed. The Persians broke into chaos as the Macedonian force plunged into the right flanks slaughtering every man in their way. The cries of agony were appalling, and the hundreds of bodies rolling into the river were turning it red with blood.

An hour later, while his wounds were being tended to, Alexander asked Parmenio for status.

"We lost no more than four hundred my King."

"And the Persians?"

"At least four thousand dead and all eighteen thousand of their Greek mercenaries have been captured and disarmed. They want to negotiate a release."

Alexander gazed upon the battlefield still being cleared. Weapons were collected and the prisoners tightly gathered and encircled by the Macedonians.

A Macedonian soldier assigned to patrol the Greek mercenary prisoners recognized one of the men he personally fought and wounded just an hour prior. When their eyes met for the second time that day, anger was replaced with respect. The Greek was sitting with one of his arms wrapped in cloth in an attempt to stop the massive bleeding, but it was soaked and he was getting weak. The Macedonian climbed off his horse and brought another cloth. He tied it around his enemy's arm and gave him water. Despite his weakened state, the Greek looked at him and nodded in gratitude. Although they were fighting to the death earlier that day, they shared an honorable struggle, leaving each with a great admiration from one warrior to another.

Then, a voice yelled to the Macedonian soldier, "You, back to your horse!" He looked up and could see all of the Macedonian guards were backing away and being replaced with armed infantrymen. He put his hand on the Greek's back and smiled, then returned to his horse. The Greek raised his hand as a gesture of thankfulness. Being a mercenary, he had a good feeling that negotiations with Alexander would result in some form of new employment with the Macedonians, which he would strongly prefer over fighting for the Persians.

The Macedonian soldier turned his horse towards his superior and asked what was happening.

"Alexander gave an order. We are all to move back."

"Are they being released so soon?"

Before he could answer, a low rumble started building from a nearby hill. The sun had already set, so it was difficult to see what it was. Then from the darkness, Alexander's full cavalry on horseback appeared. Their swords were raised and they were on a direct course for the prisoners. In a panic, prisoners on the outer edges of the circle tried to run but were met with archer's arrows.

There was nothing they could do as the cavalry slammed into the masses, trampling hundreds of men at a time. The smiling prisoner with the wounded arm struggled to his feet, but a sword struck the side of his head so hard it split his skull in half. He was dead before he fell.

With a single command from Alexander, the Macedonian brigade shamefully massacred all eighteen thousand unarmed Greeks. It was a disgusting and dishonorable act, but the soldiers carried out their orders. The screams died out as every single body was impaled again to ensure not one remained alive. Within thirty minutes, they killed eighteen thousand men that were not only unarmed, but also hoping to join Alexander's force.

The quantity of bodies, limbs and blood was overwhelming, even for a seasoned soldier.

Indeed, Aristotle and Ptolemy's concern with Alexander materialized on that day. And, as they both predicted, this was only the beginning of a long and bloody rampage.

Chapter 11

"Keep them safe."

The words dissipated into the gray. Ptolemy looked up from his bed to see an old man slowly walking away holding something close, as if he was protecting it. He called to him, but the man didn't respond and just continued walking until out of sight. Suddenly shouting pierced the silence. Through the opening in his tent, Ptolemy could see a red glow in the distance with more cries emanating from that direction.

"You're going to need this." A sword appeared in Ptolemy's hand, and Alexander was standing there, smiling. "We must go. The battle is starting."

Ptolemy thought to himself, "How odd. He so rarely smiles, except when he sees me."

Following Alexander out of the tent, Ptolemy stepped into a scene of total chaos and death. In all directions fire was falling from the sky, people were fighting each other, and blood covered the ground.

Alexander stood over a fallen King, directing his men to pierce his ankles with the tips of their spears. The King's screams were deafening as leather straps were thread through the holes in his feet and tied to a horse. Alexander slapped the horse on the rear and laughed as the King was cruelly pulled away into the smoke-filled distance.

The old man appeared again with parchments tightly clutched to his chest. With a look of sheer panic he pleaded to Ptolemy, "Don't let them burn!"

Ptolemy tried to help him when Alexander stepped in and said, "Watch this." He pulled out his sword, raised it high over his shoulder, and swung it down across the old man's chest. The sword cut deeply from his neck down to his belly, spilling blood and organs.

Ptolemy yelled, "STOP!" and then lurched from his bed covered in sweat. A guard ran into his tent and looked at him oddly.

After taking a few breaths, Ptolemy waived the guard away. He sat on the edge of the bed with his head in his hands, and tried to erase the nightmarish visions from his mind. Ever since he joined Alexander in his march across Persia, they progressively became worse.

But despite his painful dreams, when morning came, Ptolemy woke early in order to prepare for an honored event. He tried to clear his mind as he donned the formal military uniform laid out by the servants. The bronze chest plate they provided was skillfully crafted for the event and in pristine condition. When he stood over the bed to put it on, his own reflection caught his eye for a moment. Combing his hair back with his fingers, he placed the armor over his head and strapped it on his shoulders and across his chest. It glistened in the morning light, as did his blue eyes.

Later that morning, Ptolemy arrived at the top of a small hill, just above a long and beautiful valley where Alexander's legion was waiting. When he walked into the royal tent, six of Alexander's top officers were already there. They stood as men that earned their pride through years of brutal battle and hard-earned conquests.

Suddenly everyone came to attention as Alexander walked in the room. He looked each man in the eye, one by one, and then addressed the entire group.

"When our honored Demetrius fell, even the Gods bowed their heads with pride. He fought as a warrior, and died in my arms as a noble hero. And never once did he have more life in his eyes, than in the moment of his last breath." Alexander's mournful expression then turned to pride. "But tonight we honor Ptolemy, for he will now make the sacred seven whole again."

Alexander walked to Ptolemy and draped a ceremonial red cape around his shoulders and placed a single parchment in his hands. Ptolemy's eyes lit up when he realized what it was. Alexander leaned in and whispered, "I told you I would protect them."

Returning his voice to its normal volume, Alexander continued, "You have always been my friend, but now you are one of my most elite. My life and all that we fight for is entrusted to you. And truly if there is anyone that could ever succeed me with honor and wisdom, it is you, General Ptolemy."

The other men quickly surrounded Ptolemy to welcome him to the group, that is, except for one. This man had dark curly hair, an overly prominent chin, and soulless grey eyes. He turned his back and began to walk away.

Alexander shouted, "Perdiccas, what's the meaning of this?"

Perdiccas stopped, turned around with head bowed, and said, "Forgive me my King."

Such a defiant act would normally require harsh punishment or even death, but since his love for Perdiccas surreptitiously crossed both emotional and physical plains, Alexander showed restraint.

Perdiccas stared at Ptolemy defiantly, but Ptolemy calmly stood his ground. Although his eyes were confidently focused on Perdiccas, his thoughts were kept to himself – something Alexander taught him in their younger years.

Alexander walked outside with the seven closely behind. A deafening cheer from forty thousand men waiting in the valley below echoed across the landscape. Alexander waived while Perdiccas presented an exaggerated smile and kissed Ptolemy on the cheek.

While close to his ear, Perdiccas then gave a warning to Ptolemy in a way nobody else could hear. "Enjoy this moment, General. Once he's gone I'll crush you with my own hands." Perdiccas then grabbed Ptolemy's arm and raised it, which was immediately received with even more cheers by the unaware crowd.

Chapter 12

Ten years later

Carmania

A decade has passed, and killing for Alexander this long left the men physically exhausted and emotionally dismantled. Many forgot why they were still fighting for a never-ending barren desert, and completely lost all connection to their former lives, and a time without war.

Yet Ptolemy remained whole. The insight gained from Aristotle and his studies of the seven parchments taught him to separate from the illusion of life to see the reality behind it. He deeply contemplated and learned everything he could from the most horrible of losses, to the greatest of victories. He gained true wisdom, allowing his disposition to be composed and rational in the midst of death and chaos.

Alexander, however, still had the fire. One night, after their evening meal, Ptolemy sat next to Alexander and took a deep breath. "Alex, you're now effectively King of all Persia. This is something I never dreamt possible. Nobody has."

Alexander arrogantly replied, "I have."

"But what more do you need?"

Alexander looked in Ptolemy's eyes, but did not respond. He then turned back towards the East as he sat with his friend.

Despite Ptolemy's efforts, the bloody march of the Gods continued. But in the coming months, logistical problems began to grow during their continued path towards India.

With supplies dwindling, Alexander dispatched Perdiccas and a lighter unit of men to move ahead to secure food and water for the main force. Their mission was critical, but Alexander was confident in the unit and demonstrated complete trust in their success.

Five days later, it appeared the men accomplished their assignment. As Alexander's starving troops walked through Carmania, supplies were waiting. Cheers could be heard, and Alexander himself embraced Perdiccas, recognizing him for his outstanding leadership.

But it was Ptolemy that first noticed something odd with the villagers. They were not fearful, as was usually the case. In their faces, fear was replaced with an intense anger. And even after Alexander's spokesmen explained his policy of handing back control to local leadership, the people still showed nothing but total hatred.

Other soldiers started to notice this as well, but Ptolemy was the only one to consider that these people lived for five days in the unchecked company of Perdiccas.

Later that day, as Alexander bathed, the rest of the leadership sat at a long table set outside for a meal. "Wine!" Perdiccas motioned his cup towards the server, but the man just stood, glaring. Although the villager was attentive to every other order put to him, this particular one was not obeyed. "I said bring me wine you idiot", but again, no reaction. The villager simply scowled. Perdiccas stood and reached for his dagger and the villager began backing away. Laughter came from the other generals seated at the table, except from Ptolemy. His attention was in the direction that the villager was drawing Perdiccas towards. It was a horse barn, and inside he thought he saw movement from several directions, then stillness.

The villager, still facing Perdiccas, continued backing himself towards the barn while the soldiers increased their laughter and jeers. Perdiccas was enraged as he followed the man into the dark structure. He quickly took several steps in, but before his eyes could adjust, the man was gone. Perdiccas lowered his head and squinted, but couldn't see anything more than dark shapes. The horses in their individual pens were now becoming jittery, and began making noise and commotion. Perdiccas turned back towards the opening of the barn when the figure a man appeared, silhouetted against the bright light from outside. It was not the villager, but rather one of his fellow soldiers. Perdiccas called out, "Peithon, is that you?" The man did not answer.

Then suddenly from the left, a wild voice with intense anger shouted in his local Bactrian language,

"This is for raping our women and children!" The villager then burst from the darkness towards Perdiccas with a sharp spear aimed directly at his chest. Perdiccas tried to move but stumbled backward to the ground. He looked up just in time to see the villager slammed backward by a Macedonian sword. It came from the man standing at the entrance of the barn, but oddly that same man that just saved him, immediately leapt on Perdiccas and held his sword across his neck.

Confused, Perdiccas opened his eyes to see it was Ptolemy holding him down. With a growling voice, Ptolemy said, "What have you done to these people?"

Perdiccas panicked, but Ptolemy's sword pushed harder against the soft flesh of his neck.

"It was my men. They were drunk. I...I tried to stop them."

Ptolemy's controlled demeanor turned to total disgust. He finally stood and looked down at Perdiccas for a few moments, and then walked back outside to finish his meal.

Chapter 13

"Am I a God?"

After much quarreling from his troops, Alexander put their final push into India on hold to further organize the business of running such an expansive empire.

While sitting alone in the dining chamber of a large palace in Babylon, Alexander looked to Ptolemy as his friend, not as his general, for an honest answer.

Ptolemy could see Alexander's intoxicated eyes were red and becoming wet. He honestly wanted an answer, so Ptolemy gave it.

"There's so much I don't know Alex. I don't know if you're a God. But you're more than just a man - that I do know."

Alexander struggled to keep his eyes focused, and said, "It wasn't a God that fell off that boat when we were kids, was it?"

Ptolemy also smiled with that fond memory, and said, "No, that was just a boy too stubborn to duck."

"I'm still too stubborn to duck."

"I know, but look where it brought you Alex. Never again, will there be a King as great as you."

Alexander then took another long drink of wine and said in an emotion filled voice, "All I wanted was to find my empire, but the world demanded more of me."

He then raised his head towards the night sky and cried out, "Ammon! Why am I given the weight of the world, yet I still bleed? Why father? Am I not a God like you?"

Alexander's head then dropped as he moaned in pain.

Ptolemy never saw Alexander in such a vulnerable state. He helped his friend, and King, to his feet and led him to his chamber. Waiting for Alexander was a young shirtless man, who quietly took him in his arms.

When Ptolemy stepped outside for cool air, he noticed a strange glow in the night sky. Something didn't feel right. He returned to his chamber where waiting for him was his Persian wife Artakama. Although he never truly loved her, he married her at the request of Alexander to show their integration with the Persian people. That night he held her unusually tight, and without a single word, made love to her for the first time in many months.

The next morning Artakama walked to Ptolemy who was seated in deep contemplation. She stood next to him and brushed his blond hair to the side. In a gentle voice she asked, "What is occupying your mind my husband?"

After a long pause, he replied, "Alexander. I think it's happening."

Artakama knew Alexander had been very ill, and could sense the concern in her husband's voice. She knew that such a comment should not be taken lightly – not from Ptolemy. She also knew that if Alexander were to die, the world, as they knew it, would change.

"Am I at risk?"

Ptolemy stood to look his wife in the eyes, and said, "Despite what may happen, you will always be cared for." He slowly leaned in and Artakama closed her eyes, but his kiss touched her forehead and not her lips. This was more telling than anything else to the Persian Princess.

Artakama knew the promise to care for her was not a pledge of a loving husband, but one of obligation. She understood very well the great political responsibility they both had, and despite the emptiness in her heart, she had to be content with that answer.

The next day Ptolemy walked down a long and ornate hallway filled with roses and weeping people, and then passed Perdiccas who was just leaving Alexander's chamber. Their eyes met for a brief moment but not a word was spoken. Ptolemy apprehensively walked into the room. Standing on each side of the bed were priests with various ointments and incense, and two men with large fans trying to cool Alexander's fever. The young King lying in bed opened his eyes and lifted his head, but could not speak due to his extremely ailing state. He struggled to communicate until Ptolemy sat by his side and said, "You don't have to speak my King."

Alexander frowned and shook his head until Ptolemy quickly corrected his statement: "My friend."

Alexander gave a faint node and laid his head back down.

Ptolemy's eyes immediately became wet, and for the first time in his life, he openly cried. "What will become of the world without you?"

Alexander could not respond, but tears ran down his cheeks.

Before he left, Ptolemy leaned down to kiss the ring that symbolized Alexander's rule over the greatest empire that ever existed, but it was gone. Without a pause, he kissed Alexander's bare finger, and gave his King, his life-long friend, and his soul mate, one last embrace.

At the same moment, outside in the palace stables, a large black horse with a white star on his brow let out a mournful groan. In the previous days, the trainers did all they could for him, but it was not enough. The legendary horse that carried Alexander into battle, plowing through enemy lines and crushing everything in his way, was now weak and trembling in pain. The magnificent power emanating from his heart was no longer there. One of the trainers kneeled next to the horse, patted his head and neck, and gently sang to him. The horse's groans subsided with the man's soothing voice. He slowly laid his head down, gently closed his eyes and died.

The mysterious force called Alexander was gone, and in its wake was a vast empire with virtually no leader. Despite his great personal sorrow, Ptolemy knew the outcome of the next few hours would shape the political structure of the known world, so he had to be clear-headed and prepared.

The next morning, a messenger kneeled at Ptolemy's door and gave his report.

"Both General Perdiccas and General Meleager confirmed their presence."

"Good. And they agreed to the time and venue?"

"No. One wishes an additional ten days for his advisors to arrive."

Ptolemy frowned and asked, "Who said that?"

"General Perdiccas."

Thinking for a moment, Ptolemy then replied, "You can tell him I received his message, but nothing will change. The new ruling power will be established today, with or without him."

And so it began, in that late summer afternoon in Babylon, a private meeting between the three most powerful men on the planet, to determine how the largest empire ever amassed in the history of time would be ruled. In time there would be formal discussions and treaties, and regents and satraps assigned, but it was this moment that would lay the foundation of all to come.

While two of the men raised their voices and slammed fists on the table with poor attempts to force their way through power grabs, one sat with the quiet confidence of a truly wise leader.

Perdiccas proposed that Alexander's unborn son should be the successor, which coincidentally gave Perdiccas the ruling power until the boy came of age. But both Ptolemy and General Meleager quickly surmised that such an arrangement would only result in the boy's early demise, and thus disagreed. General Meleager then argued it falls to Alexander's half brother Arridaeus, but Ptolemy knew this too was an unwise proposal as Arridaeus was too feeble to rule an empire.

When his time came to speak, Ptolemy calmly explained his vision of the new world, and then summed up the basic structure: An empire divided into three major geographic regions, each ruled by one of the men at the table. Ptolemy then concluded by saying, "We will have equal seats on a council, and will meet once a year to address any needs or disputes between our territories."

Clearly threatened by the undeniable logic, Perdiccas displayed Alexander's ring, now on his finger, and said, "One ruler created this empire, and only one inherited it. The strongest." Ptolemy's eyes slightly narrowed as the bickering started again between the two generals.

With ultimate greed dissolving any hope for an intelligent discussion, Ptolemy realized there was no sense in continuing. He was the first to leave the room, and without hesitation assembled the commanders and troops most loyal to him for departure.

When asked where they were going, Ptolemy turned his eyes towards an ancient land, where the foundation of an exciting new city, named after the dead King himself was being erected: Alexandria, Egypt.

Chapter 14

In Egypt, in a temple next to the Nile River, two priests in white robes and gold jewelry were on their knees pleading to a short, stout man named Cleo. The room was highly decorated with ornate drawings and statues of the local wild life.

"Dear Sir, we beg you, please don't kill them."

"Why shouldn't I?" Cleo replied through his interpreter.

"Because they're our most sacred and holy residents. They must be protected. Please sir!"

Cleo was not affected by the emotional plea. He looked around the elaborate shrine and shook his head. "I would like to help you, but they insulted me and must be killed. It's a matter of principle."

The first priest looked to the other in confusion. In a cautious tone, the priest inquired, "Sir, exactly how did they insult you?"

"Well, to begin with, they ignored me."

"But Sirrrr, there's an explanation. It's meeeeerely a misunderstanding."

"No, there's no misunderstanding. I'm very busy and important. King Alexander himself appointed me, yet I came all the way out here and talked to them. I asked them nicely to leave. I explained this is now Alexander's territory, and it is against the rule for them to live here without my permission. And after all that, they ignored me and insulted me, so now they must be killed."

The priest quickly replied, "No, please good sir, that is not necessary. We know them very well. We have spent our lives with them, and because of that, they speak only to us."

"Oh, only to you?" Cleo chuckled. "And they do this whenever you wish?"

"No. It requires a special ceremonial process, but if done right, we can convince them to do certain things. And if we bring them some form of, well, appreciation, we have better success."

Cleo tapped the side of his leg and murmured, "Appreciation, appreciation. Let me guess, GOLD?"

"Mmmmmm, yes, oddly enough, gold seems to work best."

"So you can get them to leave if I provide this gold, right?"

"Yes, this is possible. But it can take several sessions, and there's no guarantee. Since they're so holy, changing their will is difficult, but gold certainly helps our chances." And with that the priest folded his hands in respect and bowed his head.

"Ah, I see now. Well, I'm sure they're holy as you say, and the service you provide is no doubt, very noble, but they are the ones that owe me an apology and unless I receive it, they'll be killed."

Cleo then waved to his men waiting outside with spears.

The senior priest tried to ease the situation. "Please, there's no reason for this. May I ask, exactly how were you insulted?"

Cleo answered, "I talked to them, as you do. I asked them to leave, and they ignored me. So I sent my servant to the river's edge."

Both priests looked at each other with concern. One turned and cleared his throat. "Yes, ummm, sir. Just to be sure. We....we are talking about the crocodiles, aren't we?"

"Yes, you claim to talk to them, so I did the same. My servant even brought them gold because you tell everyone that is what makes them listen to you. But then they became very rude and unpleasant to my servant."

After taking a deep swallow, the priest then asked, "Just how unpleasant were they sir?"

"They ate him."

The priests were expressionless.

Cleo once again motioned to his men who picked up their spears and started towards the river. "You can tell all the people it will be okay now. We will kill the crocodiles so they will no longer have to give their gold."

Both priests immediately stepped forward and shouted in unison, "NO!"

An hour later, Cleo was on his way back to Alexandria with a large pay-off from the priests so that he would not kill their holy, but quite lucrative crocodiles.

When Cleo entered his home, an Egyptian servant bowed and said in broken Greek, "Men are here for you."

"Whoever they are, they can wait. I'm thirsty. Bring water."

The servant left to retrieve water as Cleo ensured the gold from his rounds of 'tax collections' was properly stored in his vaults. Although his methods were unorthodox, the money Cleo raised essentially funded the building of Alexandria. Without him, the work on the new city wouldn't get done. Some, including Cleo himself, considered this talent to be part of his great financial genius, and that is why Alexander assigned him the role of funding the new city. But Cleo was no leader, and the local people had no respect for him. Unless something was done about Cleo, the local work force would simply become unavailable, and no matter how much money Cleo threw at the problem, nothing would get done.

Once the gold was secured, he then ordered his servants to bathe him and bring fresh clothes. One of the servants bowed his head, and again reminded him of his visitors. "Master, the men...", but Cleo interrupted by slapping him across the face. "I said they can wait!"

After washing himself and changing his clothes, Cleo ordered food. Sitting at his table, he smacked his lips and dropped pieces of bread and meat as he vigorously ate his meal. He then chugged a large glass of wine, which spilled down the side of his mouth. Looking around, he waved his servant to his side and then wiped his face on the servant's shirt. This was followed by a revolting release of gas from his rear as he rubbed his large belly.

More wine was ordered, but the servant behind Cleo did not respond. Perturbed, Cleo turned to slap him when instead of his servant, he saw three men standing behind him. The man in the middle was in formal military dress, and stood tall and handsome with a stern expression. When their eyes met, Cleo's face turned pale. He immediately dropped to his knees and in a shaken voice said, "General Ptolemy!"

Chapter 15

Walking alone on a sandy shoreline, Ptolemy thought of Alexander, and the absolute commitment he had for a united world. He murmured, "You were so close Alex, so close."

He continued his walk until he came upon two large boulders, both rounded and towering over his head. They seemed oddly out of place, as though the Gods plucked them from distant lands and tossed them together on the beach.

With the waves lapping at the shore, Ptolemy started to walk around the boulders, but something colorful caught his eye. Looking closer, he could see a brilliant seashell deeply wedged between the two stones. The mathematical perfection in the spiral shape, and its artistically pinkish hue was stunning. He kneeled down and squeezed his arm inside until his fingers finally reached the shell, but as he pulled, it sadly crumbled in his hand. He wondered what intelligent force could have possibly brought this delicate shell to rest between such large and formidable objects.

He examined the pieces of shell in is hand, until his eyes slightly raised and refocused on Alexandria in the distance.

He watched as thousands of sea birds scampered after the barley flour used to mark the lines where new structures were to be erected. This was not just the birth of a new city, but the dawn of a new and wonderful age. But first, there was much to be done and great forces to be dealt with. Ptolemy was also concerned with the Egyptian people. He did not speak their language, and was not considered a God as Alexander was. As the current Satrap of Egypt, Ptolemy had the authority to rule, but to truly lead he needed the respect and hearts of the people.

Later that afternoon, Ptolemy sat in the partially completed palace as he was briefed on the many building projects across the city. After the final discussion on plumbing and water distribution, he closed the meeting and began to leave when his assistant stopped him.

"Men are here for you."

"Who?"

"I don't know. They said they're under direct orders to deliver a package, and it must be directly to you."

Ptolemy merely glanced at his personal guard who, without a word, took the cue to quietly exit the room and inspect the visitors. Everyone was well aware that with Perdiccas out there, Ptolemy's life was in grave danger.

When the guard returned, he nodded to Ptolemy and then escorted the visitors in. After entering, the three men quickly kneeled and bowed heads as the man in front extended a gold box.

"General Ptolemy, King Alexander ordered this delivered to you upon his death."

Ptolemy looked at the others in the room, then slowly reached down and accepted the box from the kneeling man.

"Our most honored sir, there's something else."

"You may speak."

"A personal message from Alexander to you."

Ptolemy's expression froze, except for his bottom lip, which started to quiver. He waited to hear the very last words that would ever come from his life-long friend, and ruler. Nervous anticipation enveloped him.

"He had only three words, and they were barely spoken just prior to his death. I hope you understand."

"Tell me!"

"He said to tell you, keep them safe."

Ptolemy opened the lid of the gold box and looked inside to see old but familiar looking parchments. He stared down at them, and then looked back to the men with moist eyes. They could tell by his stirred emotions how important this was.

Ptolemy took a deep breath and gave an order, "Treat these men as my personal guests. Feed them, and provide anything they need."

That evening, Ptolemy sat at his desk and opened the box again. Using both hands, he carefully removed the parchments that an old man from Macedonia bestowed upon him so many years before. Ptolemy sat in wonderment at how perfectly these writings represented all good things the Western culture offers its people, and as he had come to learn, the same things the people of the East valued in life as well. Yes, he found different standards and different cultural aspects between the two, but the general values of people simply pursuing a good life were similar, and so eloquently portrayed in the writings. To Ptolemy, there was no greater body of knowledge to guide a leader's decisions, but his enthusiasm dissolved when he counted only five. He added the parchment Alexander assigned him years before, but there was still one missing.

Holding them tightly, he thought of Alexander, and the incredible journey they experienced over the last decade. For twelve grueling years, the young King motivated and united forty thousand men, leading them over twenty thousand miles on foot, conquering all nations in his path. Despite years of starvation and carnage, Alexander's vision and passion alone were enough to fuel the unstoppable war machine. These were the most brutal times ever experienced by mankind, yet oddly enough, with Alexander leading the way, Ptolemy always felt safe.

Alone in his room, Ptolemy was overwhelmed with a strange and painful emptiness in his chest. But this brief surrender to despair was not serving him, or his new country, so he forced his attention to a map of the Mediterranean. With no sleep, he spent the rest of the night studying the entire Middle Earth - analyzing all possible risks to his new country. He knew as her leader, he must first remove all threats, not just to Egypt, but to her bordering nations as well. At the same time he had to capitalize on her greatest potentials: wheat and sea-based trade.

Ptolemy would win the hearts of the people by addressing their safety and productivity first, giving them the freedom to pursue their own happiness and growth. By doing so, he would win their love. And with their hearts and his vision, Ptolemy was confident he could create a new age of prosperity and intellectual advancement never before experienced, and the flagship of this new era would be Alexandria.

The next day Ptolemy ordered another tour of the city, but this time he had his own agenda. Instead of the typical pitches from businesses and important men of power, Ptolemy had something else in mind.

As the entourage entered the streets, he turned to his interpreter and asked, "Where do you purchase your food?"

The interpreter immediately translated the question when Ptolemy sharply said, "No. I want to know where YOU purchase your food."

Feeling uncomfortable, the interpreter struggled. "Sir, it is not important where I..." Ptolemy interrupted and in a gentle voice said, "It's okay, tell me."

"At the market. At the edge of town."

"Good. Let's go!"

As they approached the bazaar, guards began to push people aside, but they were quickly ordered by Ptolemy to stand down. Ptolemy walked up to a man selling fruit, and said through his interpreter, "You there. What is your name?"

Averting his eyes to the ground, he replied, "I am Sareem."

"Do you have family Sareem?"

Nervously, he nodded and said, "My wife, and my son." He then pushed forward a young boy who was standing behind him. Ptolemy knelt down and placed both hands on the boy's shoulders. "You have large muscles boy. You must be strong."

In a small voice, the boy proudly replied, "I can pick up my father's sword all by myself."

"Do you know who I am?"

"Ummmmm, King Alexander?"

"No, but that's a VERY good guess!"

"Oh, I wish you were him."

The father started to shush his son when Ptolemy gave him a reassuring glance, and then addressed the boy again. "Why is that?"

"Because my father said King Alexander is a God, and protects us. Are you a God too?"

Ptolemy drifted as thoughts about the Egyptians, their belief systems and Gods began to build in his head.

Chapter 16

Syria

En route from Babylon to Macedonia, soldiers sent by Perdiccas to deliver an immensely important and ornately decorated gold carriage, were recovering from a surprise attack.

"You might feel this one." The soldier put his foot on his friend's chest, and gripped the end of the broken spear. With a sudden tug it came out of the man's shoulder. Despite immense pain, the wounded man barely grunted. After washing and bandaging the wound, the two finally had a chance to consider what just happened. Looking around, they could see only half of their men survived, and many of them were wounded.

One man sat and wiped blood from his face. "I asked him for more men."

"So, what do we do now?"

"Now? Now we go back to Babylon."

"And how will you tell him?"

"Me? No, no, not me. He doesn't like me anyway. YOU must tell him."

"Good Zeus, not me! I'm wounded, and feeling sick, I can't."

The soldier stood and took account of all the dead. "Well, looks like I'm in charge now. Let's just go. We'll figure this out when we get back."

As the twenty or so survivors gathered what was left of their belongings, they noticed five large containers of water and food that was not theirs.

"Where did these come from?" one asked.

"The Egyptians left it for us."

"They attack us, kill half our men, but leave us water and food?"

"One of them said they didn't mean us harm. They only wanted the carriage."

Babylon

By the time they reached Babylon, only twelve of the soldiers remained with the unit for fear of repercussions. The tattered group walked through the gates and into the city center. The top advisor to Perdiccas, who was crossing the same square at the same time froze in shock from seeing the early return of the soldiers, and dropped the scrolls he was about to deliver.

A short distance away in the royal Nebuchadrezzar Palace, Perdiccas, donned with a colorful robe and a gold crown, sat quietly on his elevated chair. His military leaders were seated before him in an uncomfortable silence. Each man desperately tried to avoid eye contact.

Perdiccas said, "As soon as Timoteus returns with my written orders, we can begin." A few of the men nodded, but all had blank, expressionless faces.

He then added, "I want to be notified when Alexander's body arrives in Macedonia." One man barely looked up, and then turned his empty stare downward again.

The atmosphere in the room became even more awkward as Perdiccas began tapping Alexander's ring on the hand-rest of his chair. "When Macedonia sees my gift to them, they will understand and respect the magnitude of my rule, and the power I now possess." Perdiccas scanned the room for anybody with a response, or at least some sign of agreement, but there was nothing.

"After that, our first order of business is Egypt. Three times I sent emissaries, and three times Ptolemy has ignored my orders."

One of the advisors carefully began saying, "My King, his lack of response may be...", but Perdiccas angrily interrupted.

"His lack of response is an act of treason and an insult to all of you. We must not allow the empire to be divided like this. From this point forward, Ptolemy is an enemy."

Another in the room began to speak but stifled himself. Perdiccas glanced annoyingly at the man and then continued, "I want my Legion prepared to take

Egypt as soon as possible. What little army Ptolemy still has will be crushed under our feet."

General Eumenes began to speak, "Sir." Perdiccas grimaced and the General quickly corrected himself. "My King. We still don't have confirmation that Ptolemy has defied you. Indeed Egypt is part of the empire, but even under Ptolemy's rule, it poses no risk. Time is best used in building our troops, and training them for combat. The local men have no fighting skills that we can see."

"I won't send another emissary if that's what you're saying. We'll take Memphis and Alexandria down to the ground until we find Ptolemy and all those loyal to him. Their heads will be on display for all to see. And for each of you, there will be riches beyond your imagination."

Perdiccas gave a nervous grin as he looked around the quiet room for any confirmation that his decision was a good one. "I am merely protecting the empire that Alexander has fought to build for so many years. Does anyone have any dispute with these orders or my authority as King?"

The other Generals in the room knew very well that the self-proclamation of Perdiccas was highly disputable, especially with Alexander's half brother having a valid claim to the thrown. But it would be unwise to challenge this as many men have already been killed for the slightest of disagreements since the short reign of Perdiccas. So the urge to roll eyes was controlled.

Perdiccas then added, "Once Alexander's body is returned and enshrined in Macedonia, everyone will know my ruling power and the world will be united again. And all of you are fortunate to be present to witness what will be remembered through all time, as the birth of a new God King, King Perdiccas. And it all begins with my delivering Alexander to his final home in Macedonia."

Everyone at the table looked up when the door opened and Timoteus walked in. He had the plans that Perdiccas was waiting for, but following him were two men covered in dirt and torn clothing. One had a blood soaked wrap across his shoulder, and the other a grim expression on his face, knowing the news he was about to share would not be well received.

Alexandria

In the Palace of Alexandria, Ptolemy was being briefed on the status of a most critical, yet sensitive mission he assigned to one of his regiments.

Muffled voices were barely seeping through the walls, leaving those outside very curious. A guard was struggling to hear when one of the soldiers who was on the mission chuckled and whispered into his ear. The guard immediately exclaimed, "You took WHAT?"

Inside the room, the briefing was nearing completion when Ptolemy asked, "Was there any resistance?"

"Nothing really. We had no problems."

Ptolemy nodded proudly and asked, "When will the carriage arrive?"

"Five or six days."

Ptolemy looked to his staff and issued his orders, "Begin preparations for its arrival. I want the entire city to see the procession, and I want it appropriate for a God King. In five days, we send Alexander the Great on his final journey."

Once the details were concluded, staff members burst out of the room in all directions. By the afternoon they assembled teams of people, who in turn assembled more people. Planners began designing the entire event as artisans and carpenters rushed into action. All work on buildings and other city projects came to an immediate stop in order to focus all resources on this one event.

Ptolemy instituted briefings twice a day to status progress, settle decisions, and resolve roadblocks. When any one team or any one person needed help, priorities were immediately re-arranged to ensure support was available. This hands-on approach from a leader was new to the Egyptians, but enabled much work to be done in a short time.

However, on the third day, a different kind of roadblock presented itself to Ptolemy, and this particular one was more of an irritant than anything else. After approval was granted and the visitor was allowed in, Ptolemy let out a long breath.

"What do you need Cleo?"

"Forgive me for disturbing you at this demanding time, but we're in danger of..." Cleo was interrupted midsentence when a servant entered and said to Ptolemy, "The delegate from the Sycamore province is here, do you want to see him now?"

"Upper region?"

"No. Lower."

"Have him wait."

Turning his attention back to Cleo, Ptolemy said, "You may continue."

"Yes. As I was saying, I've been reviewing our budget reserves, and my estimates show that this situation will drain...", but once again Cleo was interrupted by the servant. "The library committee is here."

Ptolemy enthusiastically replied, "Wonderful! Tell them they may enter shortly." A spark appeared in Ptolemy's eyes, but then quickly faded as he returned his attention back to Cleo.

Cleo continued, "We are...", but this time it was Cleo that interrupted himself by squinting his eyes and asking, "A Library?"

Ptolemy slowly nodded and raised an eyebrow.

Cleo shook his head and quickly made his point, "We're running out of money!"

"Ah, the city funds. Well, now that you bring that up, I've been meaning to discuss this issue with you. I have an old and very wise friend who has been concerned. So to put his mind at ease, I ordered a review of your tax collections."

Cleo's face lost a shade of color.

"It seems we have many angry people because of you. You've forced men to give over half of their earnings, and in many cases you taxed businesses into closure. You have taken properties and animals with force, and have threatened and instilled fear."

"You're actually worried about these...these rodents? You can't ever forget that they're here to serve us, and the more indebted to me they are, the easier this entire endeavor will be. I need your backing or these desert pigs will bring violence and destruction to the very streets you build for them. You must be a strong leader or..." Ptolemy stopped Cleo there.

"My PEOPLE will not be treated this way!"

Cleo finally closed his mouth, dropped his head and nodded. Ptolemy continued, "There's one other thing."

Cleo's expression froze.

"It appears eight thousand talents from your collections are unaccounted for."

"What? That's absurd! It's clearly a mistake. Nothing is missing."

"We reviewed this three times. There's no mistake."

Cleo swallowed and forced a calm reply. "Perhaps the people advising you should be reminded that I was given a great responsibility by Alexander to fund the building of an entire city. However, minor questions here or there are understandable. It's nothing to concern yourself with. I'll take care of it."

"Eight thousand talents? We could build a pyramid with that, Cleo!"

Cleo's face strained and turned red as he nervously tapped the side of his leg. "Well, there may have been eight thousand talents sequestered from the main body of funds as an emergency reserve. We must keep the capital to the levels owed to the workers, not today, but in the future or we face financial ruin. This city will never be built, and you will have chaos."

Ptolemy pulled out Cleo's records that were confiscated earlier that day, and said, "Then just show me where the sequestered emergency funds were recorded?"

Feeling trapped, Cleo then exclaimed, "I'm building a city here! I can't be questioned for every little detail of my operations!"

"Normally I would agree, but this is a very large sum. Show me where it's recorded."

"Not just anyone can...this is a complicated system. The, the records may not indicate that full amount; that is true. But, but it is in there."

"Then all you have to do is show me."

"Look, if, if I raise the taxes just a little I can have that back. These pigs won't even know the difference. Once my men collect another...", but Ptolemy had enough and nodded to the guard in the back of the room.

Shortly afterwards, Ptolemy bestowed to his people the very man that manipulated them, cheated them, and taxed them to their knees. And in a quick trial, Cleo's collections, and Cleo himself, were put to a permanent and just end.

But the true gift he would bring his people was yet to come. In a few days, Ptolemy would bring them the body of their God King, Alexander the Great, and with that, a renewed faith that this delicate seashell, their world, was in safe and worthy hands.

Chapter 17

Memphis, Egypt

A mature woman in a long linen robe named Antigone fanned herself, anxiously tapping her foot as she waited at her seat. Her husband Magas looked down at the thousands of people crowded on either side of the road. From their elevated vantage point, they had an excellent view, but the procession's route was so long they still couldn't see it all. Antigone sharply whispered to her husband, "Get down", but Magas continued to climb a decorative sandstone structure for a better view. At the top he slowly stood to take in the total scene. As he lifted his head, his eyes widened in amazement and his mouth dropped open. He murmured to himself, "Oh my dear Zeus."

The view from where they sat was just a tiny fraction of the entire event. The procession started at the entrance to the city and winded all the way to the temple at the center of town. Hundreds of thousands of people lined the entire distance of the street. He had never seen such masses at one time. On each side of the road, evenly spaced every twenty feet, were enormous and colorful clay pots decorated in hieroglyphic and Greek writings depicting the key conquests of Alexander. Brimming over the edges of the pots were giant Blue Lotus water lilies, transplanted from the banks of the Nile River. Their sweet fragrance filled the air. At various locations, large green palms were woven together with other vibrant flowers to create grand archways in which the procession would pass under. But even more striking was the winding road itself. Every square inch, from the city entrance to the temple, was covered with woven fabrics and tapestries. The rich colors of the decorated city and the great mass of people left the man watching from his perch completely awestruck.

This wealthy couple, recently from Macedonia, occupied a special viewing section reserved for the elite. With them was a young attractive woman with long blonde hair, a slender body, and an innocent and gentle face. When she saw her father pointing from his sandstone perch, she quickly jumped to her feet and in Greek said, "Oh Mother, something's happening!"

Electricity suddenly filled the air as two priests with torches climbed to the top of the city temple and approached a line of large cauldrons carefully arranged and filled with oil. The cauldron at the center was the most elevated, with the remaining cauldrons cascading down each side. The two men lit the lower cauldrons at each end and quickly backed away. The flames spread to the two cauldrons closer to the center, which in turn lit the next two cauldrons. The combined fire of all six ignited the final cauldron in the middle, which created one conjoined flame that lapped over thirty feet in the sky. The massive blaze in the late afternoon created a towering beacon for the coming entourage, and a red glow that was visible over the horizon from great distances.

Then, with the call of horns, everyone's eyes turned towards the entrance of the city. Three elephants led the procession, each carrying an ornate carriage on their back with rounded canopies. And from each carriage, women dropped handfuls of yellow and purple flower petals to the carpeted roadway below. As the elephants lumbered by, the sounds of crying began to build.

Directly following the elephants were two single-file lines of soldiers five hundred men each. They all walked in slow unison with formal military attire, including feathers in their helmets, shields, and swords. Despite emotional hardening from battle after battle, each soldier carried a grief-filled expression.

Once the soldiers entered the heart of the city, orders were shouted down the lines and in a tightly coordinated fashion they all stopped walking, removed their helmets, and turned to face the center of the road. The soldiers stood perfectly still, at attention.

At the far end, between the lines of soldiers, two magnificent black horses with long flowing manes appeared from under a palm leaf archway. The horses walked in a controlled prance raising their front hoofs high and then slamming them down to the carpeted ground with a solid thump.

Pulled by the horses was the miraculous phenomenon that everybody came to see, the body of their former ruler, King Alexander. Grief fell over the city as a large, gold-clad carriage with elaborate depictions of battles and various animals rolled into view. On each side was the inscription in several languages, Alexander the Great. Walking at each corner of the carriage were four priests, each in long white robes and carrying burning incense.

The Egyptians could only hope that their former God King was able to navigate the underworld, seeking haven in the Realm of Osiris. But here on Earth, with Alexander gone, they were vulnerable and needed a protector.

As the body passed, tears rolled over faces with hopeless expressions. The people now stood as orphaned children exposed to a violent planet with no leader and no future. Their security, their values, their entire world was about to be entombed with Alexander. Everything was lost, that is, until all eyes turned once again to the palm archway to see a tall, striking man on a horse emerging in senior military dress. He had wavy blond hair, wise blue eyes, and a proud and confident posture. Despite his clean-shaven face, he donned the physical scars of a man who fought by Alexander's side conquering nations and experiencing more than words can express. Behind him followed two thousand additional soldiers, all under his skillful command.

The young lady with her parents asked, "Who is that?" After climbing down from his sandstone perch, Magas put his arm around his daughter and gently replied, "My dear Berenice, that's the man we have been telling you about. That's General Ptolemy."

As he passed, Ptolemy glanced to the side and scanned the crowds. He gazed upward to the area where the family and other prominent citizens were located. From the masses, his eyes caught the image of this sweet young lady standing between her parents. While all the faces of the crowd were mournful and sad, hers was a soft reflection of purity and hope. Their eyes met, and in a mesmerizing moment, the rest of the world blurred.

Without taking her eyes from Ptolemy, Berenice slowly asked, "Is he Egyptian?"

"No, Macedonian." The mother then added in a coy, singing voice, "Your uncle knows someone that can introduce youuuu."

Berenice finally turned to her mother. "He's not married?"

"Well, he has a wife, but..." the father interrupted, "two". Antigone gave Lagas an annoyed glance, then turned back to Berenice and continued, "two wives, but he only married them for political reasons my dear."

Berenice thought, then folded her arms and said, "Did he love them?"

"What does love have to do with anything?"

"Well, sounds to me like he just uses people, and I'll never make that mistake again."

"No, no, my dear. This is nothing like that. This Ptolemy is an extremely important man, and has obligations you can't imagine."

"Still, if he did that, then I want nothing to do with him. He's the last man for me."

"But my sweet daughter, he's powerful and intelligent, and can give you the life you..." but Berenice cut her off. "I don't care about what he can give me! I just want a man that I love. A simple farmer or shoemaker would do, as long as he loves me and I love him."

Antigone looked at her husband in desperation, who in turn started to argue with his daughter. They didn't notice an elderly man with a white beard standing nearby and listening to everything being said. Without being conspicuous, the old man carefully observed the young lady, studying the conviction in her eyes and the purity emanating from her heart. As a realization came to him, he started to laugh so loud that the arguing family noticed and turned towards him. He quickly cleared his throat and looked away, but secretly, the wise old man produced a large, contented grin.

Chapter 18

Pelusium, Egypt

Magas and Antigone were so moved by Alexander's funeral they couldn't stop talking about it. The family was returning by boat to their farm just outside the Pelusium delta region, and not one opportunity to throw a subliminal message to their daughter was lost. "They say he could be the King of all Egypt someday, and nobody has his heart yet. Imagine that!"

Berenice tried to ignore her parents while she watched the Egyptian coastline go by, daydreaming of her future. The persistent pestering from her parents was annoying, yet deep down inside she had to admit to herself, her heart indeed skipped a beat when she laid eyes on him.

After the boat pulled into port and docked, the family was escorted to a coach taking them the rest of the way to their farm. Once there, both women went to their private chambers to refresh themselves, while Magas immediately looked for his farm hands. The lead of his crew approached, as he usually did, with two horses pulled behind him.

The men mounted the horses and began their methodical walk through the crops - something Magas insisted on every time he first arrived. The fields of flax were flowering, blanketing the entire hillside in bright blue flowers, gently waving in the Egyptian breeze. Magas took a deep relaxing breath, and sighed, "Beautiful."

But the loyal worker next to Magas was not as content. He shamefully lowered his eyes and pointed to another hillside of crops in the distance. Magas shielded the sun from his eyes and looked.

His heart dropped in disbelief.

While her husband was out, Antigone prepared food and was setting the table when another of the workers named Karpos walked into the ranch-house kitchen. Not knowing the family had returned, the dirty man politely bowed and began to back away when Berenice stopped him. She began to invite him to stay and eat when her mother loudly cleared her throat and pinched her nose. Berenice giggled, but still motioned to the man to stay. Without anybody to translate, she had to use gestures alone.

When Magas returned, Antigone immediately sensed something was bothering her husband. "What is it?"

"They did it again."

Antigone's expression froze. "The water?"

Magas painfully nodded. "This time they blocked the larger channel. It's dry, and crops are dying." Dropping his head into his hands he moaned, "Oh why, why are they doing this?"

Knowing how important the flax was to Antigone's linen business, tears now fell from the eyes of both women as they embraced him.

The worker also knew how devastating this was to the family, and felt crushed. Magas looked at him and softly said, "Karpos." The worker understood enough to know he was just asked to leave. The family that pulled him from poverty and trusted him with their farm was in crises. After stepping outside, Karpos took one last look at the family he loved so much, and then climbed on his horse.

The crew leader that previously escorted Magas through the fields sharply called out in his native tongue, "Karpos, no!" But Karpos didn't stop. "Karpos!" he called out again. "You'll get yourself killed!"

Karpos ignored the warning and kicked the sides of the horse until it galloped out of sight.

Chapter 19

Alexandria, Egypt

As the tour finished, the team of designers and engineers anxiously awaited Ptolemy's reaction. With Alexander's body properly entombed in Memphis, the people of Egypt were now eager to serve their new leader, and the palace in Alexandria was their next best opportunity. At just twenty percent complete, it was already a stunning structure.

Although he was excited and felt like shaking everyone's hands, Ptolemy maintained the persona of an aloof ruler, giving just a subtle smile with the briefest of nods. While his controlled response maintained the respect each man felt for their leader, it also expressed just the right level of appreciation, fueling their passion.

After Ptolemy left, the group relaxed and began speaking freely. One man happily said, "Did you see his eyes? He was pleased."

Another answered, "Yes, he definitely was. And this is good knowing what he wants next."

"The library?"

"Yeah, and a big one. I heard he's talking of something the size of a small pyramid."

"Jobs and food for us and our sons, men", another blurted out. "But what's a library anyway?"

"I don't know...it holds things."

"We can use it to hold all the gold we make building it!" a voice in the back yelled, making the room laugh.

Outside, Ptolemy chose to walk back rather than use the carriage waiting for him. As arrangements with his personal guards were made, Aristotle approached and politely asked as he always does, "Mind if an old friend walked by your side?" Ptolemy chuckled to himself because he knew he was the honored one walking next to such an intellectual giant.

Aristotle quickly made his point. "We have a situation at the river."

Ptolemy stopped walking and gave his full attention.

"Farms in the Pelusium region were in danger the last few days. It appears a man named Karpos was sabotaging water systems that diverted river flow into the area."

"Did he do any serious damage?"

"Yes, but nothing that can't be repaired. The soldiers have him now."

"So why bring this local issue to me?"

"Well, as usual, there's more to this. I don't believe Karpos is a random madman. He was born in that area. He's a skilled builder, and even helped construct the very dikes he was harming."

Ptolemy cocked his head back and said, "Well that doesn't make sense. I need more information."

"I knew you would." Aristotle motioned to a woman who was walking behind with Ptolemy's personal guards. She quickly ran and joined the two men. After a long curtsy, she stood straight but kept her eyes lowered. "This young lady believes she has some insight. Her family recently purchased farms in Pelusium, and has employed the man."

Ptolemy waited until her head slowly lifted, and her green eyes finally looked into his. He warmly asked, "What was the name?"

Aristotle replied, "Karpos?"

Ptolemy shook his head, "No. Not Karpos."

"Ah, yes, of course, forgive me. My dear friend, this...this is Berenice."

If Ptolemy had not been lost in the lovely vision before him, he might have recognized the devious inflection in Aristotle's voice. It was last heard many years prior at the foot of the Aegean Sea, when Ptolemy was introduced to a young boy destined to rule the world. He didn't hear the inflection, or the construction occurring all around them, or the powerful waves crashing on the nearby rocky shore. But he did hear her name, and each syllable was sweet music. Be-re-ni-ce.

Ptolemy also didn't notice Aristotle promptly leave after the introduction. Instead, he focused on every word that cleverly danced from her lips.

Berenice, conversely, remained focused on her personal mission. She felt the man wreaking havoc with the Nile water system had a good reason, and must not be executed without being heard. But time for that was running out.

After brief pleasantries, Berenice began to make her plea. "My family hasn't been in Egypt for long, but ever since we arrived we employed Karpos. His family had a farm in the nearby area but lost it. So we took him in, and gave him employment. This is completely out of character for him, but the soldiers will not allow us to speak on his behalf, and refused to delay his execution. They won't listen to anybody."

"The soldiers will do as I say, but I can't just overlook the grave nature of this man's actions. The water supply is simply too vital to allow this to go unpunished." Seeing the disappointment in her eyes Ptolemy took a deep breath, and then asked, "Is there any chance he's not responsible for this?"

Berenice lowered her eyes and sadly answered, "No. There's no chance."

"Why do you do this then? Do you care that much for this man, to stand by him so?"

"You think I do this for him?"

He looked at Berenice with sincerity in his eyes.

She nodded and continued, "Yes it's true. I do it for him."

A disheartened expression grew on Ptolemy's face. "He has your heart then?"

"My heart? No. Nobody has my heart."

"But why then? Did you bear his children?"

Berenice raised her hand to her mouth and chuckled. "I think I should tell you something about Karpos. He's foul, he's irritable and he smells. I could never care for him, and we have no relationship in ANY way except through employment."

Hiding his relief, Ptolemy asked again, "Then why?"

"I believe an outside influence has reached the local government, and if it is not addressed, the problem won't end with Karpos. Land owners can't afford further issues with our water."

Ptolemy took great delight in the young lady's logic. He began to reply when his servant approached and whispered in his ear.

Ptolemy stepped to the side to speak to him in private, and then promptly left with the other guards.

The conversation ended so quickly Berenice didn't know what to think. She looked at Ptolemy's servant now standing next to her, and asked, "What happened?"

The man bowed his head and said, "General Ptolemy has ordered I bring you to his palace tonight as his guest."

Berenice then slowly conceded. "I see. Of course, I should have known. He wants to finish this conversation tonight, in his private chamber."

Confused, the servant clarified, "General Ptolemy was called to an emergency meeting with his military. He ordered me to personally ensure your safety and comfort while he's gone. I'm to provide for your every wish, and I assure you - you will have your own bedchamber. Please, it is important you come with me."

A private palace, outside Alexandria

Ptolemy's guards escorted him to a carriage that eventually carried him to the outskirts of Alexandria. In the late evening, they arrived at a secret location, where a small, secluded palace was sequestered for an urgent meeting. When Ptolemy walked in, his top military advisors were already there, waiting for him. Everybody stood then quietly sat, except Nikomedes. He remained standing with a painful look on his face.

"General, we thank you for coming, and trust you will understand why we must forgo pleasantries. What you're about to hear is not my voice, or the voice of the men in this room. It is the combined voice of all soldiers whose allegiance, hearts, and very lives belong to you. We fought by your side for twelve years under Alexander, and would have taken a sword for you without hesitation."

Ptolemy quickly replied, "And I would have taken that same sword for any of you."

With an emotional voice, Nikomedes continued, "Yes, yes we know. We also know that when Alexander died, you brought us out of Babylon and gave us a new life without war - without death. Many of the men are taking wives and building homes here. And that is why," the man swallowed, and then continued, "that is why...this is so hard to say."

Ptolemy stood and said, "Niko, you must speak freely."

Looking directly in Ptolemy's eyes, Nikomedes finally completed his statement. "We want you out of Egypt, and we're prepared to use force if necessary."

Chapter 20

Sakhmet's Prison in Egypt's Upper Basin

In a crowded and sweltering room, a man leaned against the wall wiping sweat from his face. There were no windows, no benches, and only warm, soiled water to drink. With each breath his lungs choked with hot, stench filled air. After so long in these foul and stifling conditions, the man's mind was in a deep, timeless haze. As a scuffle broke out in the center of the room, it barely caught his attention. He just slowly hobbled away, stepping over a man that collapsed earlier that afternoon and hasn't moved since.

Then, through the dull insanity, a familiar name was heard. The man's eyebrows raised and then lowered again. The name was heard again, "Karpos," and this time his eyes partially opened as he realized someone was calling his name. But before he could raise his head, two hands reached under his arms pulling him to his feet and quickly ushering him out the door.

Handing Karpos a cup of fresh water, the guard continued what he was saying. "If it were my call, I'd be throwing your ugly ass in a sack and tossing it in the Nile, but seems you have a friend." Turning to the guard next to him, he ordered the prisoner placed in a more tolerable facility.

The next morning, guards escorted Karpos to a small interrogation room where he was told to sit and wait. Although Karpos was thankful for the change of conditions, when a higher-ranking official entered the room, he still grimaced.

The official took note of this reaction as he slowly sat. The two guards in the room started towards Karpos to administer punishment for his disrespect, but were quickly waived off by the official. He then grinned at Karpos, and in a controlled and polite manner said, "It seems we have not been introduced, you and I. My name is Sakhmet, and this is my facility. I trust that your evening was more comfortable than the previous arrangement we had for you."

Karpos grunted angrily.

"Well, some people have difficulty expressing appreciation. So...perhaps we talk about the reason you're here. I understand you have much history with our water system."

Karpos only scowled as Sakhmet waited for a response.

"Hm-hm-hmmmm. Well, this is certainly not a good start." He took a deep breath, and then continued, "How about we start with what I know? I was told that you engineered many of our dams and waterways, and have become quite skilled in this profession. Your life has been dedicated to this cause, and for this I commend you. Your countrymen commend you. But yet, you return in the night, like a rodent, and attempt to destroy the very systems you built. I'm puzzled."

After receiving no reply from Karpos, Sakhmet continued. "Yes, puzzled indeed. So now you're here, as my guest, and you have my complete attention. Please, help me understand this."

Karpos just shook his head.

"Hmm. I see you're not in a mood to talk with me, but this...this is a problem, and I was so looking forward to a pleasant conversation." Sakhmet twisted his neck to the side and continued, "Maybe it's time I explain a few things about me. Despite what you may have heard, I'm not the ill-tempered man people talk about. I take good care of those under my watch, and I always encourage an open dialogue. For example, just a few days ago, I was attempting to talk with one of the other men, but like you, he simply wasn't in the mood. I thought fresh air along the banks of the Nile would help, but as it turned out, it was the local wildlife that eventually opened him up." Sakhmet leaned forward. "You know those crocs are amazing creatures. They twisted his arms completely off before ripping into his belly and taking him down."

Karpos sat motionless as Sakhmet leaned back and continued. "Ah, and then there was Ptah. He was of a similar nature, and not interested in conversing with me at all. I took him to see our wondrous desert, but still nothing. So I finally decided a closer view would help. I tied him and buried his head in an anthill. You know, I think he may have changed his mind about talking, but sadly, his muffled screams were too hard to understand."

Karpos quickened his breath, but didn't show any other reaction.

"So this now brings us to our little mystery named Karpos, which I have just been ordered to solve. You've been charged with attempting to disrupt our water system, and my men tell me you're simply crazy and should be drowned in the Nile. But you know, I just don't think it's that simple. I think there was something you were trying to accomplish. Do you have a response to any of this?"

Karpos lowered his eyes and chuckled.

Sakhmet also chuckled, "I don't understand this reaction. But no matter, I'm confident you will answer all my questions. You just need to get started. Here, let me help you." He then grabbed Karpos by the hair and slammed his head on the table. Blood immediately poured from his nose and mouth. Then, in a low voice, Sakhmet slowly spoke in his ear, "My men will rip the skin from your face, do you understand? Now, you were caught dismantling one of the dikes in the region, were you not?"

Karpos moaned in pain, and then mumbled, "N-n-not, manting."

"What was that? I couldn't hear you. Please, again."

Karpos cleared his dry throat and struggled to get the words out, "Not dissssmantling."

Sakhmet's eyes squinted as he loosened his grip on Karpos.

Babylon

Six hundred miles to the east, in Babylon, the citizens were learning more about their new leader, Perdiccas. Although the title of "King" was not clearly established yet, he allowed people to refer to him as such, and at times, would even insist on it.

One of those that had something to learn of her new leader was a woman named Lila, who ran a fruit stand in an outdoor market with her daughter, Sadira. Lila's husband was imprisoned for failing to meet the new tax demands implemented by Perdiccas, but every sale from the fruit stand was one step closer to buying her husband's freedom back.

In the early morning, Lila was setting fruits out for display as she always did with her daughter, but today, in particular, was an exciting day. Lila sung out to her daughter, "Just one more day Sadira, and we might have enough. I think today is the day!"

Sadira put her hands together in excitement. "Then daddy can come home?"

"Yes, daddy can come home! But we must sell a lot. So I need your help. I want you to be extra friendly to the people, and talk to them when they walk by."

Excited to help her mother with the sales, the young girl clapped her hands and happily exclaimed, "Okay! I will get us a lot of customers!!"

As the morning went by, Sadira cheerfully greeted everyone and asked if they would buy her fruit. With innocence in her voice she would ask, "Would you like to try my apricots? They are fresh and the best tasting ever!" Lila was pleased with the sales, and was busy taking payment from a customer when she noticed some commotion in the street. She looked up, and a feeling of dread instantly came over her. King Perdiccas and five of his bodyguards were walking by. Everyone on the street lowered their heads as he passed, except one excited little girl hoping for a big sale.

Lila called out, "Sadira, no!", but it was too late. The little girl ran to Perdiccas, and asked, "Would you like to try my apricots?"

Perdiccas stopped to see who dared address him in such a direct manner, only to see the girl standing in front of him. He leaned back to his interpreter, who in turn translated. Perdiccas then looked back towards the girl. She had long beautiful black hair and bright eyes. Her hair draped over her white linen dress, which was wrapped tightly around her mid-section. She was holding out a small basket of apricots. One of the bodyguards started to push the girl aside when Perdiccas stopped him. "Wait! Let's see what we have here."

Perdiccas looked back at Sadira and said, "So, you want me to try your fresh little apricots?" Perdiccas winked to his men as they all laughed. He then motioned for the interpreter to step closer. Lila, fearing her daughter was in danger, also approached with her head lowered, but a guard put his hand out and stopped her.

"Yes! They're the best!!" the girl cheerfully replied.

Perdiccas reached down and slowly rubbed his fingers over one of the apricots as he leered at Sadira. "How old are you girl?"

"I just turned twelve. Do you want to try my..." Lila quickly interrupted, "No!"

Sadira looked back at Lila and finally saw the concern on her mother's face. She then felt fingers touching her neck. It was Perdiccas, now on his knees next to the girl. He brought the girl's hair to his face, took a deep breath, then stood and said something to one of his men. Turning back towards the girl he tossed her an apricot and she caught it. Laughing again, Perdiccas said, "See, she loves me and wants to marry me!" The men all laughed again.

A guard then knocked the basket from Sadira's hands and grabbed her arm. Lila cried, "No!" and struggled to pull her daughter back but was shoved to the ground. She could do nothing but watch the men pull her daughter down the street. Deafening cries of "Mommy, HELP!" and "My girl, they're taking my girl!" echoed through the streets.

Crying hysterically, Lila was helped up by other venders in the area. She tried to run after her daughter but was held back for her own good.

Three hours later, the same little girl who started the morning so bright and innocently trying to sell fruit to help her father return, slowly walked back to her mother's fruit stand. Her expression was lifeless, and she was in complete shock.

Lila screamed, "Sadira!"

She ran and hugged her daughter, but Sadira just stood there traumatized, with her arms at her side. The top of her dress was torn, she had bruises on her arms and face, and the lower part of her clothing was bloodstained. Her innocence stolen forever, the girl started to shake, and then finally broke down into a heart-wrenching cry.

Alexandria, Egypt

As men continued their work on the royal palace, Aristotle sat in one of the newly completed rooms quietly reading when Ptolemy came in. Using his teacher's own words, he asked, "Have time for an old friend?"

"Ha, my boy! I have endless time for you."

"As do I for you teacher."

Aristotle immediately noted something in Ptolemy's tone that was concerning. "Is all well?"

"I have much to think about, and wanted to talk."

"Well, fortunately talking is my favorite endeavor next to thinking. Tell me, what occupies your mind?"

Ptolemy pulled a chair out and sat. "It's Alexandria."

Excited by the topic, Aristotle chuckled. "You know, when I hear you speak of it, I'm so delighted my boy. Your vision is far surpassing that of Alexander's trading port. It will literally be a breeding ground of dreams and knowledge, and a beacon for all to follow. I feel for the first time, humanity has a chance."

Ptolemy barely nodded.

"But this is not the heavy weight on your mind is it? Why do you not jump for joy as I do? Speak to me."

Ptolemy gazed down at a small gold object in his hands, and then said, "My men want me to leave Egypt."

"What?"

"They want me out, and they will force me if they have to."

"Absurd! Your men love you. What reason did they give?"

"Exactly that. They want to protect me." Still looking at the gold object, Ptolemy continued. "Three times now Perdiccas has ordered me under his ruling power, and three times I rejected him. He wants Alexandria, and he's building his legion to come take her. But this seashell will crumble in his hands."

Aristotle responded with resolve, "You can not allow it! Perdiccas is a tyrant. You must protect Alexandria from him."

"Agree, but by doing so, I will be launching all of Egypt into war."

"Then so be it! Nothing is more important, not even our lives. Fight to your last breath for her, and then keep fighting."

Again, Ptolemy gazed down at the gold object. When Aristotle looked, he quickly recognized it as the pendant Ptolemy wore when he was a boy. Given to him by his mother, it was a reminder of her love. It was then that Aristotle's brilliant mind realized the source of Ptolemy's apprehension. He put his arm around Ptolemy's shoulders and said, "You were young you know. There was nothing you could do."

Ptolemy closed his eyes and could see his home exactly as it was during that dark night, so long ago. It was the night he was attacked by the two men, only to be saved by his young friend Alexander. The same sick feeling came over him as if he was still there. Ptolemy remembered how after the attack he was bloodied and severely limping, but Alexander was by his side helping him walk. Together they hobbled through the dark night to check on Ptolemy's mother. When the stone house came into view, it was dead silent, and all animals and birds in the immediate area were still. With every step a feeling of dread and loss grew in his chest.

As the two boys approached the home, they could see the front door was slightly ajar. Ptolemy looked at Alexander and slowly pushed it open. In the middle of the main room, his father Lagos was on the ground holding his wife's limp body in his arms, lightly stroking her hair. When Lagos looked up his face was filled with so much anguish he was almost unrecognizable. Ptolemy's knees gave out and he dropped to the floor. As Alexander stepped forward, Lagos completely broke down and let out a long, mournful cry.

Returning from his painful memory, Ptolemy said in an emotion-filled voice, "I couldn't even save her...how can I save Egypt?"

Aristotle contemplated the question and then said, "The answer may be closer than you think." Reaching into the pocket of his robe, he continued, "I want you to think about Macedonia, Alexandria, everything that has happened, and everything that is happening now." Aristotle then put his hand on Ptolemy's back. "Remember what I taught you years ago my son." He placed an object on the table and left the room.

Ptolemy looked down to see two shiny stones, tightly pulled together.

Chapter 21

The Nile River, Alexandria

Arriving in the mid-afternoon, Berenice anxiously waited by the river's edge for her second meeting with Ptolemy. But this meeting would be much different than their first, just a few days prior. She spent the last several hours with servants preparing for what they promised would be a luxurious boat ride down the Nile.

Now, nervously waiting at the dock, Berenice could barely stand the anticipation. "When will it be here?" she asked a third time.

"Soon, soon."

After a long and painful hour of waiting, a boat finally appeared in the distance. And within a few more minutes, the small, run-down vessel with torn sails flapping in the wind approached. The boat was steered into the dock and quickly secured. A rickety plank was tossed down and Berenice was taken on board. Waiting for her with his political worries deeply buried, was Ptolemy, standing proudly to welcome her.

As she stepped aboard, a handrail broke in her hand almost causing her to fall, but Ptolemy's strong grip caught her and held her tight. He then led her to the front of the boat where there was a small, crudely assembled table with two chairs. When Berenice sat, the chair creaked and the table rocked back and forth due to uneven legs. The boat was an old fishing vessel and thus reeked of dead fish.

Everything was so dilapidated it almost made Ptolemy snicker, but he kept it well hidden from Berenice. Instead, he focused his sharp blue eyes directly on hers. "As you can see, my boat has been cleaned for your arrival. If I had wine, I would offer you some."

Mesmerized by his eyes, Berenice hardly noticed what he said. She just replied in an intoxicated way, "It's absolutely lovely."

When Ptolemy asked Berenice about her previous home in Macedonia, she became energetic again, speaking fondly of her parents and her childhood.

"Why did your parents bring you to Egypt?"

"Because of the wonderful new city we heard so much about."

"Oh really? What exactly did you hear?"

"Oh many things! But most of all, we heard Alexandria would be the center of world trade."

"You did?"

"Yes!!" Berenice became even more excited. "But want to hear something even more amazing? I heard they might build a great library, larger than any ever built before! And did you know they're planning to build an enormous lighthouse too, so ships from all over the world can find us?"

Chuckling, Ptolemy said, "Yes, I may have heard of such things."

After realizing whom it was she was talking to, Berenice put her hand to her mouth in embarrassment. She mumbled under her breath, "I guess that wasn't very smart of me, was it?"

"I think it was innocent and sweet. I think you are sweet."

The only member of the boat's crew approached Ptolemy and kneeled. "Forgive me for interrupting, but is everything satisfactory sir?"

Ptolemy replied, "Yes, this boat served its purpose well," and then winked.

"Then shall we proceed as planned?"

"Yes, absolutely."

With that order, the boat was steered to another dock at the river's edge where an enormous ship was waiting, at least five times the length of their current boat. It was magnificent, with flowers, torches and luxurious blankets, furs, and furniture. Twenty servants were waiting on-board with their arms folded behind them.

Berenice asked, "Whose is this?"

With a slight grin, Ptolemy extended his hand and led her to the dock, and onto the new ship. Immediately servants were by their side, escorting them to the upper deck. Waiting was a luxurious table of rare wood, fully set with silver and gold, ready for a King's meal. Around the deck were candles and small torches illuminating flowers and fabrics meticulously placed just for the right effect. Beyond the ship was an enveloping 360-degree view of the Nile, blending into the deep-red sunset sky.

As the ship quietly glided on the water, thousands of torches lining each side of the Nile were lit in sequence, one after another. Their reflection danced in Berenice's eyes as the light extended far into the distance. Then, from an unseen place on the ship, the melody of a harp slowly emerged so gently it was hardly noticed at first. Ptolemy was proud at how well his people answered his order. "Make dinner an experience that will live forever in her heart."

Standing at the bow of the ship with Ptolemy close behind, Berenice leaned back and let out a long and comfortable sigh. "Have you ever seen anything so majestic?"

Ptolemy wrapped his arms around Berenice and held her tight. "I've seen things you could never dream possible. An entire city carved out of stone. A temple altar built purely from gold. I have stood at the top of mountains higher than the clouds, where the sky was so expansive, you would think you're looking into the very eye of Zeus." Ptolemy turned Berenice around to face him, locking his eyes on hers. "But never before has my heart come so alive, as when I look at you." Berenice then felt Ptolemy's strong hands pulling her tight as he passionately kissed her. Without a conscious thought, she found herself in a complete state of surrender.

Inside his arms, Berenice was warm and safe. With her head resting against his chest, she closed her eyes and slowly became aware of his heartbeat. She let out a deep breath and whispered, "How is it I can feel this way with you?"

Kissing the top of her head, Ptolemy replied, "Feel what way?"

"Like I'm the only woman in Egypt."

Ptolemy warmly replied, "Because you are, in my eyes."

Berenice snuggled closer to his body and then looked up into his eyes. "I never felt so good, but so scared at the same time. I feel the person I was is fading away forever, falling into a bottomless abyss, and there is no return."

"Don't be scared. I'm here to catch you." Berenice could feel Ptolemy's strength and confidence. Holding her even tighter, he added. "For as long as you let me, I'll take care of you, and keep you safe. I promise."

The ship continued to gently sail with torches lighting its way. The food came and the two ate as they talked and laughed. Although Ptolemy enjoyed her sweet innocence, it was Berenice's clear logic and eloquent language skills that delighted him most. There was no pause in their conversation. It flowed freely, like the Nile into the night.

But beyond all the words and physical feelings, was a magical chemistry that transcended all. It was a total emersion of desire and contentment, love and lust, fear and bravery. It was everything, all at once. And just as Ptolemy ordered, the memory of that evening would live forever in their hearts.

The beaches of Alexandria

In time Ptolemy and Berenice were inseparable. As Ptolemy solidified his vision for Alexandria, Berenice faithfully stood by his side, ensuring that her future King was taken care of and loved. Although they lived in the capital city, Memphis, the future Alexandria held their hearts and was the breeding ground of their dreams.

One early morning, Ptolemy and Berenice were walking along the coast in Alexandria. This was the coolest time of the day, and something they both came to enjoy whenever they were there.

Berenice usually started the conversations, and this morning was no different. "Tell me about Alexander my love", she said as she picked up a pink seashell.

Ptolemy searched for a place to start, "It's not easy for me. He was such a big part of my life, for so long."

"Aristotle said he was your friend when you were boys."

"Yes...long ago."

"And when you became older?"

"As we became older, things changed, and quickly. Alexander became important to many people, and suddenly, there was a line just to see him. Always the line. But despite that, he was still my friend. I wish he didn't leave us."

"But my love, you're the Satrap of all Egypt now."

Ptolemy didn't answer and just looked back towards the city.

By this time most people, including Berenice, were aware of the threat that hung over Ptolemy and Alexandria. She knew this is what occupied Ptolemy's mind so she snuggled into his arms, laid her head against his chest and said, "I've been hearing things."

"Oh you have? What have you heard?"

"Mmmm well, I heard you ignored messages from Babylon. Messages sent by King Perdiccas."

Ptolemy kissed the top of Berenice's head, "This is not something for you to worry about."

"Maybe not. But why don't you at least talk to him?"

"Talk to Perdiccas? To what end?"

"To find out what he wants. Maybe he just needs to know you're not a threat."

"You want to know what he wants? He wants Alexander's empire, that's what he wants. And he'll take all the riches of Egypt and force its men into servitude to make that happen. There will be no library, and no future. I can't let that happen."

Berenice's tone became serious. "I heard we don't have much time. I heard that he built a large army."

"He has. And he has General Eumenes. But Alexandria must not fall into his hands, or it's all over."

"But why? Why is it so important? Why can't we just leave and find some other place to be safe?"

Ptolemy held Berenice even tighter and spoke from the depths of his soul. "My love, if I were to let my heart guide all I do, we'd already be far away by now, probably raising children in some small village by the sea."

Berenice melted at that thought. "Oh...that's my dream, and all I ever wanted. Please tell me more about it."

"More about our lives? Well let's see...first of all, every day would be completely carefree and full of sunshine. And did I mention children?"

"Yes, you specifically promised children, and I must inform you that for me, one or two simply would not do. So how many do you see?"

"Oh, dozens at least. In fact our home would be so crowded we'd have to sleep in a big pile at night - all of us, even our dogs. But in the morning we ride horses through green fields, and at sunset we walk the beaches and greet the stars as they come out. I teach my sons to fish and hunt, and surround my wife with beautiful fabrics, fresh flowers and kisses every day."

Berenice giggled, "And I would make my husband big and fat from all my cooking."

Ptolemy warmly chuckled with her, "I'm sure you would. And that would be all a man could ever want. But we must never forget that Alexandria is bigger than what my heart wants, or yours. Alexandria is not just about our world, or that of our children's. It's about everyone's world, of all countries, for all ages to come.

Alexandria is how we can show the Gods that we are not their children anymore. That we are ready to end war and hatred so we can learn and grow, and create our own destinies. For so long I've seen brutality and death so sickening it still haunts me, but now...now, we are close to leaving that all behind, forever. Oh Berenice, I can see it as if it's right in front of me. It's a library so immense that it has everything ever written, no matter what country it comes from. All beliefs, all observations, all theories, all facts. And there would be no bias placed on them, no matter what their origin. All knowledge of the entire world at our fingertips. And men with great minds like Aristotle's will come from all over to study, share, debate, and develop understandings you can't even imagine possible."

Ptolemy then somberly looked down and finished, "But Perdiccas will end that dream, unless we can stop him."

Berenice's heart filled with admiration for her man as he spoke with such passion, but in her youthful way she decided the mood needed changing. She ran to the water with mischief, cupped her hands and splashed Ptolemy. She then let out a playful shriek as he laughed and chased after her.

When Ptolemy caught up, he hoisted her into his arms and spun her around. He was about to toss her into the water when her bright green eyes intervened. He paused, and then kissed her instead.

Slowly setting her down but keeping her close, Ptolemy came to a realization. "When I'm with you my love, my world is timeless."

Chapter 22

Sakhmet's Prison

In the far upper region of Egypt, a special envoy arrived for a second time at a prison to discuss a certain inmate.

In a small room, Sakhmet sat across a table from a Macedonian officer sent by Ptolemy. "Captain Lykos, I can appreciate that you're following orders, but the last time Ptolemy questioned me about this Karpos, it was simply a waste of time. I only kept him alive at the direct order of Ptolemy himself. Prisoner Karpos will never amount to anything of interest. I should have killed him when he first arrived."

Captain Lykos pointedly stated, "You were ordered to learn his motives, and you had much time to do so."

Sakhmet bitterly laughed. "Motives? From a lunatic?" He then nervously wiped his brow. "It was quite a while ago when he was last interrogated. But from what I remember, it was all gibberish. He was destroying our water system for no reason."

One of Sakhmet's guards then interjected, "Sir, he said he was just returning water that was stolen."

Sakhmet looked at the man with irritated eyes and flippantly added, "Fantasy - all fantasy."

Ptolemy's officer took note of the exchange and asked, "Is this true?"

"True? Families farmed here for generations, and never had water problems. He merely used the dikes to steal water from his neighbors - it's that simple."

Another Macedonian soldier leaned in and whispered something to the officer. Captain Lykos nodded and then formulated his next question. "You've done an excellent job Sakhmet, and I will report your progress to General Ptolemy. But I'm curious about something. If for generations the farmers have never had water problems, why all of a sudden would there be a need to steal water now?"

Sakhmet's outward confidence waned. Knowing that his secret was close to being revealed, he swallowed again. Sakhmet knew very well that water was being diverted, and received a fair amount of gold for looking the other way. And since the family that employed Karpos did not participate in such bribery, their water was cruelly denied.

Sakhmet, frustrated he was not allowed to kill Karpos two years earlier, defensively replied, "I have no idea. He's insane, and I'll put him to death right away."

Captain Lykos harshly snapped back, "Ptolemy's edict has not changed. If he dies you die. Bring him to me, now."

Chapter 23

On a grassy hilltop above a valley, a trader and his son were dismounting their horses to make camp after a long day of traveling. They left Alexandria five days earlier, heading towards Babylon to conduct business. The tired man groaned and then muttered, "Tie the horses and find the food we packed." Rubbing his rear end he added, "My old ass is sore already," but the boy didn't move. He just stood looking over his father's shoulder into the valley below. "Nicolas, did you lose your hearing? I said tie the horses!" Again, there was no response from the boy.

"Nicolas?" The father slowly turned around to finally see an enormous black mass of soldiers blanketing the valley in the distance, heading their way. He never saw so many men at one time. He shivered at the sight and his mouth dropped open. Stumbling back, the man's mind was spinning.

The boy turned to his father with concerned eyes. "Father, who is it?"

"I don't know, but this is not good. Nicolas, load'em up – we leave now!"

"Where to?"

"Back home. They must be warned."

Alexandria

Four days later, the news of the sighting reached Ptolemy. Although the approaching threat was fully expected, the final news made him think again about his vision for Alexandria, his values, and the people he was now responsible for.

A voice from the entrance to his chambers came. "Sir, the men are here for you." Ptolemy barely nodded in response. He continued his reading for several minutes, then rolled the parchment and carefully placed it in his gold box. After taking a deep breath, he rubbed his eyes with both hands, and then slid his fingers through his hair combing it back from his face. He walked out of his private chamber and down a long hallway until he reached the military situation room, where fifty of his top men were waiting for him.

Ptolemy centered himself in front and wasted no time. "Not long ago, you gathered together in what many would consider an act of betrayal. And in no uncertain terms, you demanded I leave Alexandria. Had this order been given to King Alexander instead of me, you would all be dead by now." Ptolemy began to walk as he slowly continued. "But what others call treason, I call an act of loyalty. I know you wanted to protect me." Ptolemy paused occasionally to look into his men's accepting eyes. "But you were gravely mistaken my brothers. Your love is misplaced. Our lives, our futures, and everything you and your children will value, is in Alexandria, not me."

Ptolemy then broke the news in his direct fashion. "The time we have dreaded is now upon us. Egypt is under attack."

A jubilant voice from the room echoed out, "General Ptolemy – we don't dread this. We're soldiers. Glory will be ours! We will sharpen our spears and reinforce our walls." Another voice yelled, "We will lay traps, and we will fight. Their dead bodies will decorate our streets!"

Everyone cheered but Ptolemy. When the room quieted, he then corrected his men. "We will not devise traps, and we will not re-enforce our walls." Confused looks began to grow on the faces as he continued, "Alexandria is too valuable to put at such risk. Do I need to remind you of the devastation war can leave behind? Have we not destroyed enough cities? And have we not lost enough loved ones?"

The expressions on the men changed while a voice asked, "If we're not to defend Alexandria, then what are we to do?"

Ptolemy once again squared himself in front of his men. "Listen carefully. What I'm about to say shall not leave this room."

The men carefully listened as Ptolemy steadied his thoughts. Despite the unbelievable weight this one man carried on his shoulders for his new country, he still couldn't help but think of the woman his heart literally ached for - a woman, who, over the last two years, made his life more fulfilled than anything he had ever experienced. This fight was not just for Egypt and Ptolemy's dream called Alexandria; it was for the love of a woman that transformed his already amazing life into a majestic gift from the Gods.

The Royal Baths

As Ptolemy issued orders to his men, Berenice was at the far end of the palace, preparing herself for a bath. Standing in the private royal bathing chamber, she poised her body like a Greek statue, allowing her white linen dress to softly fall from her shoulders. Long blond hair gently danced across her back as she stepped into a golden tub lined with beautiful mosaic tiles. Unaware of the extreme situation faced by Ptolemy, her mind was free. She leaned her head back and closed her green eyes, allowing her senses to fully appreciate every sensation.

The gold was flawlessly smooth against her skin and the oils and flower petals in the warm water released an intoxicating fragrance. A female servant, wearing a transparent wrap that exposed one breast, stood behind Berenice slowly pouring warmed water from a vessel to rinse her hair. The light from carefully arranged candles penetrated the mist, softly illuminating white hanging fabrics designed to surround Berenice in warmth and sensual beauty. But when the sound of the water echoed into the corridors beyond, Berenice noticed a dark, male figure lingering in the shadows.

The female servant set the water aside, picked up another vessel of heated scented oils, and carefully lifted it over Berenice. Drops of warm oil were now falling on her cheek, and neck. Knowing she was being watched, Berenice allowed the rhythm of the drops to bring her body deeper and deeper into a state of ultimate sensitivity. Carefully guided by the servant, the drops slowly migrated to the top of her shoulder, pooling at her collarbone until it finally streamed down between her breasts. Without a conscious thought, Berenice's hands were now caressing her own silky-smooth legs.

Taking another deep breath, sensual anticipation enveloped her entire body. Overtaken by the sensation, Berenice moaned and slightly opened her eyes to again see the male figure still watching her. As she looked up, the figure stepped closer, causing a soft beam of candlelight to shine on his face. Although his features were still indiscernible, there was intensity in his deep eyes that never once strayed from Berenice's. She moaned again as the man approached the bath. His leather armor dropped to the floor, and his feet stepped into the water. In complete surrender, Berenice felt the man descend upon her with a strong and deliberate force. As the oil dripped on his back, he grabbed her hair and passionately kissed her mouth. When Berenice finally pulled back to take a breath, the sight of Ptolemy's face and intense eyes sent a loving jolt directly into her heart, waking her from the misty dream.

From her bed, Berenice was confused as she woke to reality, but as consciousness returned, so too did the ache in her belly. Then suddenly, the sound of footsteps filled the courtyard below Berenice's window. Looking down, she watched the officers from Ptolemy's army quickly leaving his briefing room. She could sense something urgent was happening. A few minutes later, a voice came from the door to her room.

"Forgive me. May I enter?" One of Ptolemy's most trusted servants was standing there.

Berenice quickly ran to him, "What is happening? What do you know?"

The servant shook his head and replied, "All I know is General Ptolemy has just issued his orders."

"Are we preparing for war?"

The servant stuttered. "I don't know....maybe."

"Where is he?"

"That is why I was sent. He wants you to contact your mother and father, and collect all your personal items."

"Are we leaving the city?"

Lowering his eyes in disappointment, "It would appear so. But I really don't know. There could be enemies in our city, so his orders must be kept secret for now. They won't tell me more than this."

Berenice began to lose her breath. "But, but I don't know if my father and mother are home. When is Perdiccas coming? What do I do?"

The servant quickly tried to put her at ease, "Please, don't worry, you'll be safe."

"But what of Alexandria? Is it really over?"

"No, no. Alexandria will always be here."

Knowing the servant lacked the facilities to understand the gravity of the situation, Berenice left it at that. But once alone, she fell onto her bed and cried.

As servants were sent for Berenice's parents, she began a frantic search for all her gems and other items she could personally carry. Her eyes then fell upon a very special sapphire ring from Ptolemy to celebrate the start of a new life together. Her head slumped as fear and emotion began to overwhelm her. Tears began to form when two strong arms wrapped around her from behind and cradled her tightly. Normally she would have been startled, but her longing senses already recognized the warm and reassuring presence. Ptolemy's soothing voice said, "Don't worry my love. Don't worry."

Berenice placed her hands over Ptolemy's arms, closed her eyes and leaned her head back on his chest. Even in the face of total devastation, she never felt so much love and security before in her life.

"The time is here my love. You must leave me now. My men are here to take you and your family to safety."

Berenice quickly turned around. "And what of you? When will you follow?"

"No my love. No." Ptolemy had a look of reassurance on his face, but red emotional eyes.

"But you must come with me!"

Ptolemy just shook his head again and swallowed.

"You can't do this! Alexandria or not, your people need you alive...... I need you!"

Ptolemy looked at her face with the wise words of Aristotle echoing in his head: "Perdiccas will never stop. If you love her, you must leave her."

In a low voice, Ptolemy whispered in Berenice's ear, "It won't end with me. He'll destroy everything and everyone close to my heart." Bringing his eyes to hers, he then choked on the final words that had to be said, and that she had to hear. Just six simple words, yet even as he spoke them, they stabbed into his own soul like a cold steel knife, "You need to let me go."

Berenice's emotions exploded. "No!" She slapped his face so hard his head turned to the side. But without turning back, he looked to his guards at the door who took the silent cue to pull Berenice from his arms. Ptolemy shut his eyes as the woman he loved with all his soul was carried away in tears.

Chapter 24

Nile River, at Heliopolis

After years of failing to make Ptolemy submit to his rule, Perdiccas finally ran out of patience. As a result, a formidable legion of twenty thousand men was assembled with two orders: Take Egypt, and kill Ptolemy.

To ensure secrecy, Perdiccas killed dozens of citizens for merely having knowledge of their mission. And after they departed Babylon, life under his command became even worse.

Knowing what he was capable of, his men lived in fear of his maniacal mind, but after months of traveling, they finally approached the Nile River at the outskirts of Egypt, and a renewed energy grew among the ranks. The next four days were spent searching for a place to cross the treacherous waters.

Emerging one morning from his tent, Perdiccas quickly confronted two of his generals, Peithon and Antigenes, who came to present status. "What did you find?"

Peithon replied, "We believe the new guide is not as familiar with the river as we hoped. Once again, we believe it is far too wide and dangerous to cross here."

"Is this not where the guide said we can cross?"

Peithon replied, "Yes, it is."

"Is this not the third such attempt?"

"It is my King."

"Then get the guide, and take us to the river now."

By the time they arrived, the sun sat low in the horizon making the bank across the river just barely visible. Looking into several hundred yards of dark turbulent waters, Perdiccas turned to the guide. "You brought us here to cross, right?"

Painfully contemplating his mistake, the guide replied, "Yes, but I don't recommend this particular place my King. I..."

Perdiccas interrupted him. "You brought us here, did - you - not?"

"Yes my King, but, but the river appears to have changed. We cannot cross here."

"Nonsense! You told us you were the expert guide, so why would you lead us to the wrong crossing point?" The guide froze in fear until Perdiccas finally shook his head and said, "Get out of my sight."

The guide dropped his head in relief and let out a long breath. He started for his horse when Perdiccas had a change of mind. "Mmm, before you go, I'm thinking you deserve a special honor."

The guide stopped, looked to the two soldiers and swallowed.

"Yes, I'm thinking with the wonderful service you have provided, that you should be the first to cross. Or, would you prefer to stay and explain why you led twenty thousand men, their supplies and equipment including horses and war elephants, to the wrong location?"

Contemplating his options, the guide took a deep breath, and then slowly walked to the muddy shoreline. With one last glance back towards Perdiccas, he removed his clothing and stepped into the water.

Within just a few steps, the ground dropped out and he was struggling just to stay afloat. Choking on river water was unpleasant, but nothing compared to the fear of what lurked below or worse yet, the fear of an angry Perdiccas. The sinister Nile churned into the night as its shadowy waters concealed horrific dangers. The guide was near panic as he swam into the darkness, thinking of the crocodiles that normally waited for prey by the shores. With the strong current pulling him down stream, he committed every ounce of energy to moving forward.

After what seemed to be an endless fight, the guide was taking in more water than air. Exhaustion and lack of oxygen was too much. His head began slipping below the surface when his feet finally touched something solid.

Crawling through the reeds and onto shore, he was completely spent. On his hands and knees he coughed water from his lungs, but once able to stand, the guide's thoughts turned back to Perdiccas. Knowing that his mistake would not go unpunished, he staggered away into the night.

On the other side of the river a soldier reported back to Perdiccas, "My King, we believe he made it."

Perdiccas nodded his head and concluded, "Well then, we cross tonight."

"But my King..." the soldier was interrupted when Perdiccas raised his hand.

"I know what you're thinking. You fear the dark waters, and you ask yourself, how can our men swim against the pull of the river?" With the elephants in his peripheral view, Perdiccas continued, "Where you see barriers, I see solutions. But of course I can't expect men of inferior intellect as you to understand, so just do as I say."

Instead of consulting with his men, Perdiccas decided on his own that elephants would be sufficient to ensure his men and horses could safely cross. Perdiccas issued his orders, and soon the elephants were brought into the water, forming a safety net from shore, all the way to a small landmass midway across. And just as Perdiccas predicted, the sheer weight of the elephants was enough to keep them in place against the strong currents. Once the last elephant was situated, a commander then ordered the first of his men to start their crossing.

A young man in the first platoon named Timo solemnly stared into the darkness. Never being a good swimmer, the tales of evil currents and hungry crocodiles sent fear down his spine. At least with an enemy clearly in his sight, and a sword in his hand, Timo had a fighting chance. But in front of him now was an invisible and cruel enemy. Without taking his eyes off the river, Timo nervously asked the man next to him, "Have you ever done something like this before?"

Nikolaus gave his younger nephew a reassuring response. In a warm and confident voice he replied, "Just a little midnight swim my boy," but deep down inside, fear ripped at him as well. And worse than the fear of his death, was the fear of his nephew's death; allowing his sister's only son to be killed during something as meaningless as a river crossing, as opposed to honorable battle, would be an unforgivable violation of her trust.

Reassured by his uncle's confidence, Timo followed Nikolaus into the dark waters. But with each step, the pull of the river current grew, and like the hands of death, it was constant and unforgiving. Once the water level reached Timo's chest, water viciously splashed in his face, causing him to choke and cough.

Being a much larger man, Nikolaus still had solid footing and continued his pace, while his struggling nephew fell further behind. Eventually the water became so deep, Timo's feet began slipping on the river's bottom. Panic set in, and his arms flung wildly against the current, accidentally dislodging his sword, which quickly disappeared in the murk. "Uncle!" Timo called out, but with all the river noise and trumpeting elephants, Nikolaus could not hear him.

Instead, Nikolaus sent words of reassurance back to his nephew, who was sadly no longer there. "Don't worry, we're getting closer. Only think of the other side. That's your target, and nothing else exists. You'll make it!"

Remembering his sister repeating twice, "This is my ONLY son," Nikolaus shuttered at the thought that her boy would die while placed under his care. When he looked back, he then realized his worst fear: Timo was gone. He frantically called out into the darkness, but there was no reply.

Fifteen yards down river, Timo's body slammed into the line of elephant's, where despite his exhaustion, he managed to hold onto an elephant's harness. The mahout on top of the elephant saw the young man struggling for his life, and quickly untied a leather strap and lowered it as a lifeline. "Take it!"

Timo saw the strap, and knew this was his final chance to live. With the little remaining energy he had, he reached out for it, but lost his grip and his body was ripped away by the water.

Timo fell into mental shock and gave up. The splashing stopped as his limp body completely succumbed to the river's force, flowing into the blackness, and into the powerful hands of Death. But then suddenly, Timo felt a strong tug backward, and water once again viciously rushed around him. Without understanding how, Timo then felt his body hoisted in the air, back towards the leather strap, which he quickly grabbed and wrapped around his hand.

Keeping the promise he made a year before, Nikolaus offered a trade that night, and Death politely accepted. As Timo recovered from atop an elephant's back, his uncle was pulled away into the evil dark waters. And in all the confusion of the ill-fated crossing, Timo would never know that it was his Uncle Nikolaus that saved his life that night. But that was not important. What was important was that a man's word was kept, and at least there was one mother in these violent times whose ultimate trust would not be misplaced.

After dozens of other men were pulled down the river to their deaths, the crossing was stopped. Perdiccas stood at the riverbank, watching elephants being turned around and surviving men stumbling back to shore. He snarled as he bitterly spit on the ground.

Sakhmet's Prison

Early the next morning, deeper in the desert, guards at Sakhmet's prison followed the orders given them and released Karpos from their custody. They watched as Ptolemy's men walked the prisoner towards their horses, put him on a horse and rode off. One of the prison guards said to the other, "I never thought after so long they'd come back for him."

The other added, "Yeah, that's Macedonian logic for you. First we catch a criminal and they order us to keep him alive. Then they send men for him? What are they thinking?"

"I don't know. You'd think the ruler of all Egypt would have bigger worries than some lunatic that plays with water."

"ENOUGH!" Sakhmet blasted at the two guards, who were not aware of his proximity.

Nile River, at Heliopolis

By now dozens of bodies from Perdiccas' failed crossing were found along the river bank. The guides pointing them out to Ptolemy who respectfully knelt down to get a better look. He shook his head with disgust as he noticed many more limbs and other unrecognizable parts lining the shore.

The morning light silhouetted an Egyptian soldier standing next to Ptolemy. "Crocodiles," he declared.

Ptolemy was sickened that Perdiccas would be so careless with his own men. Without hesitation he issued his orders, "I want all of these remains properly cremated and returned to their families." Standing up, he then addressed his entourage. "Do you all see this? These soldiers didn't even have the honor of dying in battle. Never forget. This is how he treats his own."

On the other side of the river, in his tent, Perdiccas barely looked up when his military advisor entered. "We acquired three new guides my King."

"And?" he painfully replied.

"They all agreed the Nile is too dangerous to cross here."

Perdiccas slowly shook his head in disbelief that such an obvious statement would be made. "Where's Eumenes?"

"He was summoned as you ordered my King. In just three days we'll have another crossing point, but there's better news. There's an Egyptian base we should consider. It's lightly fortified and will be completely caught off guard. With General Eumenes, it will be our first victory at essentially no cost to us."

"Does Eumenes agree?"

"Yes my King."

Perdiccas finally stood and said, "Fine, so be it." After looking into the distance, he then ordered, "From this point forward, we travel only at night. Ptolemy will have no warning of the beast about to slash his throat."

The advisor nodded in agreement. "Wise my King. There will be no advance notice. And even if there was, he will look for our attack from the wrong direction. By crossing further down the river, we bring the surprise."

Perdiccas silently agreed and the plan was so ordered through the ranks. The legion of soldiers continued their march into the dark dessert until as promised, on the third night, a distant glow of a military camp across the river came into sight.

"Fort of Camels," the lead guide declared.

Perdiccas snickered to himself, "Like the desert snake we come." The moonlight shined off his bronze armored chest, yet his hate-filled eyes were black as the hole in his heart. He issued orders for his entire legion to make camp. They had a few short hours to prepare for their first battle, but in the meantime, there were to be no fires and no sound. With their presence hidden in the dark of night, not a soul would be aware of the impending attack, that is, except for a young man hiding in the reeds near the water.

Rami was one of many local Egyptians ordered on a clandestine mission by Ptolemy to scout the river's edge for signs of an approaching enemy. And tonight, fate wisely selected him. Rami quietly scampered to his small reed raft and paddled to the other side.

Ptolemy looked into the silent night knowing that his mortal enemy was out there somewhere. Like Aristotle's stones from Magnesia, the forces of Perdiccas and Ptolemy were being drawn together for an ultimate destiny.

Nearby, Rami's raft made it to shore. He quickly found an interpreter and approached one of Ptolemy's most trusted officers, Stephanos. After being told of Rami's sighting, Stephanos immediately approved a briefing directly with Ptolemy. To ensure all information would be reported accurately, he pointed to Rami and ordered, "Bring him."

Rami's eyes opened wide. This would have been a special honor for any man in Ptolemy's legion, but for a fifteen-year old Egyptian boy, this was unfathomable.

The small entourage including an interpreter walked to a nearby cluster of large rocks where Ptolemy was sitting with his senior advisors discussing options. As they approached, three men stood in a defensive posture, but recognizing Stephanos, they backed off.

Having everyone's attention, Stephanos tilted his head toward Rami, but Rami froze with apprehension. Frustrated, Stephanos grabbed Rami's shoulders and squared him in front of the still seated Ptolemy, but the fifteen year-old immediately dropped to his knees out of respect. Losing patience, Stephanos quickly picked him up again and cleared his throat loudly.

Rami took a deep breath and swallowed, then nervously began to describe all the details of what he saw. Feeling intimidated, he never once looked directly into Ptolemy's eyes, and when done, he looked at Stephanos who gave him an approving node.

Ptolemy stood and asked, "Did they see you?"

Rami confidently shook his head, "No."

Ptolemy looked at the others then returned his attention back to Rami, taking note of his young age. With pride he said, "Well done. What is your name boy?"

The interpreter allowed Rami to answer this one directly. He said, "Rami."

Stephanos then spoke up, "They're heading for the Fort of Camels."

Ptolemy agreed. "Notify the guides and pass the orders down. We leave immediately. We must get there first."

Stephanos and Rami left, but another officer that arrived with them stayed behind. He fought with Ptolemy for many years in Alexander's force, and earned the privilege of speaking openly. "His estimates may be low you know."

Ptolemy gave his full attention.

"The scout said Perdiccas brings an army twice our size, and war elephants. But this was only what he saw. There could be more."

After waiting for the question, Ptolemy then realized the point and put a hand on the man's shoulder.

"Your concern is heard my old friend. But never forget this is our Egypt now, and we're one with her people. Yes he brings an army, and he brings elephants. But don't forget they must first cross our sand, and after that, our river. I don't care how many he brings."

The officer didn't fully understand, but accepted his leader's judgment. He nodded and started to leave when Ptolemy stopped him. "I'm curious. Where did you find this Rami?"

"We didn't. He found us."

Ptolemy, always wanting to understand what motivates his people, probed further, "He barely looks old enough to hold a sword."

The officer chuckled, "He's not. I remember this one well. He wanted to join our army to fight for you, and bring glory to his family. We almost turned him away, but after convincing us he knew the river better than anyone else, we allowed him to come."

"It was a good decision. Growing up with Alexander, I learned to never judge a warrior by age or size alone. As for Rami, let's give him bigger shoes to fill and see how he does, shall we?"

"Yes sir!" The officer walked away completely impressed that Ptolemy continued to think of leadership development, even in the most stressful of times.

Chapter 25

Fort of Camels

Flanking each side of the river, both opposing legions traveled throughout the night in the same direction, but only Ptolemy was fully aware of the situation. Based on intelligence gathered, Ptolemy's army raced all night towards Fort of Camels to defend it from Perdiccas. Perdiccas, however, was unaware that his new objective was compromised. His expectation was to reach the area by morning, cross the river, and effortlessly take the fort.

Perdiccas pushed his men through the dark desert for many hours until finally a glow from across the river appeared. Then, other elements began to fall into place. Reports came in that the river was extremely shallow and easy to cross at this point, and other reports indicated the fort was lightly fortified. So the decision was made and orders were quietly passed down the lines, from platoon to platoon, to put the men into the proper configuration for an attack.

As light of early dawn slowly emerged, the natural colors of bronze and yellow began to blanket the dessert. It was a stunning site, but the only color the waiting soldiers saw was red. The twenty thousand men under the rule of Perdiccas were mentally prepared for the slaughter. Their muscles flexed, their sweaty hands gripped swords and spears, and fifty-two war elephants donned their harnesses and leather protection.

Knowing the fort offered little resistance, Perdiccas ordered four of his regiments forward, fifteen hundred men each, with the remaining fifteen thousand held back in reserve. With one lone archer standing by his side, Perdiccas nodded his head and the archer leaned back and released the flaming arrow across the early morning sky.

The quiet dawn suddenly roared to life as the first set of platoons began crossing the river at its shallowest point. Leading the way were twenty powerful elephants carrying a crew of mahouts on their backs, with men on the ground flanking their sides.

Observing from a safe distance, Perdiccas turned his black eyes to the unit commander. "How many fled the fort?"

"None," was the response.

"Nobody?"

"Nobody, my King."

Perdiccas was pleased, thinking they were not spotted yet.

However, inside the fort, a panicked commanding officer shuttered at the thought of charging elephants now sloshing their way across the Nile. He turned to Ptolemy's scout who only warned him of the impending attack just twenty minutes earlier, and slammed him against the wall. "When will Ptolemy be here?"

The scout had no easy answer but to push out the words, "I don't know, but soon. You just have to hold them until he's here."

The Egyptian officer, who never fought in actual battle, finally faced the true source of his dread: his own lack of experience. He released the scout and gathered his thoughts. Straightening his uniform and turning to his servant, he said, "Tell Awan I want him to assemble all the men immediately. Go. NOW!"

Minutes later, addressing the fort's garrison of one hundred and sixty five men, the commanding officer went straight to the point. "By sunrise, we will be under attack."   The men were stunned at the news, but listened as he continued. "However, our King's forces are coming. All we have to do is survive until then. You trained for this day, and your bravery will be remembered. That is all."

The men found no inspiration in his words. They had a weak leader incapable of decisions under pressure, and they were merely a figurative presence, not a hardened defense by any means. Standing against any serious attack would be suicide without Ptolemy.

In a final symbolic act of abandonment, the officer turned his back to the men and returned to his quarters. The garrison needed leadership, but faced a closed door of a spineless man instead. After a brief moment of confusion, Awan seized the moment and assumed a position of command.

"You heard him. We need to hold this fort until Ptolemy's forces arrive. I want the entire wall manned.

Find all the weapons you can and line the perimeter. Now! Hurry!"

Most responded to Awan's orders except for a small group of nine. Instead, they formed a circle and began to huddle. Awan impatiently looked at the group and yelled, "You! I said go to the wall!"

A few of the men looked up and then back down again. Recognizing one of them, Awan snapped, "Tor, what is this?"

One of the men took a step toward Awan and defiantly declared, "I have no issue with you Awan. But this is suicide. You think Ptolemy is coming? You think he can save you? Then you wait for him, and you can die for him too. We're leaving." Tor then turned around to address the garrison. "We're going. Who's with us?"

Awan quickly barked back, "No! If we divide, it will be death to us all." Having no time to deal with insolence, Awan immediately withdrew his sword and readied it by his side. The group of dissidents saw this and reached for their weapons while two other soldiers quickly ran to backup Awan.

Despite the tense standoff, Tor kept his back to Awan, slowly pulling a knife from its sheath. Once free, he nodded to his comrades and then suddenly turned to attack when Awan's sword sliced through the night just in front of Tor's face. The blade's pass was so silent most thought it was a miss, but Tor froze in place while his expression changed to grief. His knife dropped from his hands as he reached for his neck. Blood poured through his fingers, his knees buckled and he fell to the ground from the fatal cut across his throat.

Awan's complete commitment to keeping his garrison together as a unit removed all resistance from the remainder of the men, and soon the entire perimeter was manned.

Once again, silence fell upon the fort. Awan and the others all focused on the impending attack, studying the filtered morning light, looking for any signs of movement from the direction of the river.

Seventeen long minutes passed when a deadly sound emerged from the distant gray - the trumpeting of elephants. Awan yelled for his men to ready themselves, but commotion from the rear of the fort caught his eye. Awan jumped from the forward wall and ran to the back of the fort, where dozens of soldiers were showing signs of distress. When he arrived, he peered over the back wall to see another attacking force in sight and just minutes away.

The men turned their panic stricken faces to Awan for orders, but he simply held his hand up as he continued to assess the situation. Suddenly he shouted, "Open the back gate!" but his men hesitated, so he shouted even louder pointing towards the back of the fort, "OPEN THE GATE!"

The gates opened as ordered and the men prepared for the attacking wave, but instead of bracing, Awan climbed to the highest point on the back wall and raised his spear to the sky. Puzzled looks surrounded him, but all questions were answered with one jubilant word that was roared from his mouth as loud and as long as his dry throat would allow, "PTOLEMY!!!!!"

Jubilation spread across the fort like fire, as so did the thunderous sound of the approaching horses of Ptolemy's men.

Seconds later Ptolemy rode through the gate, dismounted and immediately looked around. Without hesitation, he ordered stacks of supplies and equipment to be moved to make room for the two thousand men still arriving. He then turned back to those manning the rear gate.

"Who's in charge here?"

Eyes turned to Awan.

Seeing that Awan was not wearing the uniform of a fort commander, Ptolemy quickly concluded that Awan was filling a void, and nodded to him with pride. But time was limited, so Ptolemy immediately took charge.

Whether Egyptian or Macedonian, it didn't matter. Every single soldier within the walls of that fort knew who was in command now, and they responded to their leader without hesitation and with ultimate trust. Ptolemy ran to the front of the fort, and issued orders in all directions to all unit leaders.

The fort was made of simple wood leaving it vulnerable to breach, so men with swords and spears were sent to the center, giving them immediate access to any potential break. Archers were ordered to the forward walls, but before any further strategy could be devised, the regiment from Perdiccas finally appeared over the horizon.

As archers hurried into place, unit leaders assisted while keeping one eye on Ptolemy. In less than a minute, Ptolemy, now standing on the forward wall with his back to hundreds of his archers, raised a hand up high. All archers pulled their bows back, loyally waiting for the final signal. Then, as the dense mass of attacking soldiers came into range, Ptolemy thrust his hand forward and a wave of arrows from behind the fort sailed over his head and blanketed the sky. Their flight path was a spectacular high arch, landing directly in the middle of the charging platoons. But after several volleys it was clear they would not have a significant impact. Some men fell, but the attacking mass was too great in numbers to be slowed and continued building speed and energy.

Ptolemy wiped the sweat from his eyes and jumped to a higher perch on the wall to assess the situation. Seeing that the lead attack elephant was just fifty yards from the main gate, Ptolemy called out, "Spears forward!" but in all the noise and commotion, only a few platoon leaders heard the orders. Around the other two sides of the fort, most of the archers never received the order to step back, blocking the soldiers armed with spears from defending the impending breach. With the elephants pounding the ground and thousands of soldiers bellowing out their battle cry, Ptolemy's orders and those of his platoon leaders were being muffled out. The lead elephant, now at full velocity, was just ten yards from the vulnerable fort.

"Spears!" Ptolemy yelled again, and then a third time, but it was in vein. So he quickly picked up a spear and ran to the front wall of the fort. Seeing this visual cue, his men finally knew what he wanted, but it was too late.

As the enemy closed in from all sides, Ptolemy's soldiers rushed to defend the fort's perimeter, but the archers were still in the way causing men to stumble and fall. Time slowed for Ptolemy as chaos surrounded him. Disorder like this never happened under Alexander's command, but then again, a defensive posture was never required in his campaigns. The men were simply not trained for this.

Suddenly with a thunderous crash, the lead elephant smashed the front gate and violently stomped through the debris. At the same time in all directions, the enemy was climbing over the perimeter walls and dominating Ptolemy's men who were still trying to find their footing. Painful cries filled the air as hundred's of spears began to pierce the bellies of Ptolemy's archers.

The harsh reality pushed Ptolemy's mind inward as a brief vision came to the forefront. Sitting in the garden next to his teacher, young Ptolemy asked inquisitively about leadership in the midst of hand-to-hand combat. A warm breeze gently swayed the olive tree next to them, making the golden light of the late afternoon dance upon their faces. Aristotle replied, "In such extreme times, when all the planning and strategy is over, the true enemy is indecisiveness. When the mind fails, allow the animal inside to take over. It will know what to do."

Clarity quickly returned to Ptolemy as a man was slammed to the ground just feet from him. The stunned soldier made eye contact with his King and reached out his hand, but the enormous pad of a crazed elephant smashed down upon the soldier's head, crushing his helmet and skull with a single crack. As blood sprayed through the openings in the crumpled helmet, Ptolemy grabbed the fallen soldier's spear and stepped back towards the perimeter wall.

His men were being killed in all directions and Ptolemy's mind was spinning. Finally, taking his teachers advice, he took a deep breath and allowed a burst of power from within his chest to explode. He yelled to the two men nearest him, "Follow me!" and ran directly back towards the massive elephant that had now trampled seven of his soldiers. The angry beast flung his trunk wildly from side to side throwing men in all directions. Ptolemy could see his soldiers trying to dodge it as they attempted to kill the men on the elephants back, but it was impossible for them to get close enough. Another soldier was slammed by the trunk and lofted in the air, while hundreds of attacking men continued to rush into the fort from the opening the elephant created.

Undeterred by the frenzied combat that ensued around him, Ptolemy focused all his attention on the massive beast instead of the men it carried, targeting its only vulnerable spot. When he lunged forward, his two men followed, loyally fighting off attacks from either side. After ducking the deadly trunk twice, Ptolemy seized a brief opportunity and plunged his spear deep into the elephant's eye. The frantic wailing of the elephant was deafening as it lurched back, causing its two front legs to tower over Ptolemy, who instinctively tried to run but stumbled and fell. He looked up from the ground to see two massive pads looming fifteen feet over his head, but instead of crushing down on him, the elephant reared back with so much momentum it went completely over, smashing the crew it carried. Several more of Ptolemy's soldiers immediately jumped in to finish the kill.

Seeing the ultimate commitment of their King's warrior heart, and the massive elephant going down, the other soldiers became invigorated and a combined energy ignited among Ptolemy's men. Fighting side by side with their leader, they became fearless.

Dozens more men ran toward the crashed gate engaging the enemy as they entered. The very men that Perdiccas expected to effortlessly take the fort were being beat to the ground with a relentless pounding of swords and calloused fists.

Other breaches in the perimeter were now being defended with the same results. Ptolemy's men swarmed with such power and fury that they simply crushed the attacking soldiers.

On their own initiative, one of Ptolemy's platoons ran through the main broken gate and surrounded two other war elephants outside the fort, killing them and the men they carried.

With his lead elephants down and hundreds of his forward men wounded or killed, Perdiccas finally sent the order to retreat.

By the afternoon, the little fort that was first thought to be easy prey stood in proud defiance. Perdiccas had no choice but to order his remaining force back to regroup. His legion, still formidable and still far outnumbering Ptolemy's, had to be preserved in order to take his ultimate goal: Alexandria.

Perdiccas shuttered as anger coursed through his veins.

Chapter 26

Alexandria

Walking among stonecutters and carpenters still working on parts of the royal palace, Aristotle thought about Ptolemy's dream of a magnificent library: the combined knowledge of the entire world at his fingertips. There would be hundreds of thousands of scrolls and books, carefully cataloged and stored, and great scholars collaborating in the many conference rooms, sharing ideas and debating theories. It gave Aristotle chills when thinking about it, but the chills soon turned to a dull pain deep in his chest. As he stepped over a young man and his master fitting small tiles into a beautiful mosaic on the floor, he ached at the irony that war will decide the fate of such an inspiring institute of peace.

"Teacher!"

When Aristotle turned to see who called, his eyes lit up. It was Berenice, but the sweet innocence that he observed at Alexander's funeral just a few short years before was no longer there. Instead, her face was determined and serious. In a short time she had become more like a Queen than any he had ever known.

"Hmm, I should have known his servants were not enough to keep you away. Your beauty is only surpassed by your persuasiveness, my dear."

Berenice ignored the compliment and remained solemn.

Aristotle began to assure her in his gentle and wise way. In a warm voice he said, "I've known him since he was a boy you know, and in all of his wondrous life, he has never loved a woman as he has you."

Berenice slowly shook her head, "Then he should have known I could never live without him. If something happens..." Aristotle quickly shushed her and put his hand on hers and squeezed. With tears now streaming from her eyes, Berenice cried, "Why? Why does it have to be him?" She glanced at the doorway and continued. "All those people outside barely know him, yet they walk in his streets, and bathe in the safety he provides. All their arguing and bickering about petty things, yet at this very moment he fights for their lives. I use to love them. But now...now I despise them."

"No my dear, you mustn't. They don't know what's happening, and the bitterness you hold will serve no purpose."

With her head down, Berenice nodded in agreement and murmured, "My last words to him were in anger, and all he showed me was love. I feel so ashamed of myself." Berenice buried her face in her hands and continued crying.

"There my dear, your reaction is understandable. And I understand your feeling of wanting to be with him, but as our King, this is his burden now, and his alone. Even if you were there, his concern for you could easily be his downfall. It's best this way."

Berenice fell into Aristotle's arms where she was consoled and gently rocked. He closed his eyes and pondered Ptolemy's small chance of victory, and concluded that indeed, she was not safe in Egypt. Straightening her in front of him, he took a deep breath and said, "I need you to listen to me not as your King's advisor now, but as your friend. Go and gather your mother and father and let his men take you to safety."

"And what of you?"

"Don't worry about me. His men have orders for your protection. You have no choice in this my dear. Now get your parents before it's too late and you're forced to leave them behind."

Berenice wiped her tears and started to say, "But I can't live without..." when Aristotle quickly interrupted again. "It's what he wants. Do it for him, and for your parents." And with that, Berenice finally nodded in agreement.

Aristotle watched as Berenice was escorted towards her parent's home by two of Ptolemy's personal guards. For much time her mother and father stayed at the Royal palace to be near Berenice, but eventually relocated to a smaller palace Ptolemy built just for them. As they traveled through the streets, she could see panic growing in the city as word of the impending doom spread. All work on the buildings had stopped, and most everyone had their arms full of belongings, running in all directions. To Berenice, it was surrealistic and sad, like the premature end of a sweet dream.

Once the carriage stopped at her parent's home, Berenice ran inside. Both parents were distraught as she explained why they had to flee. Magas put his hand to his mouth, and then turned to his wife. "Take Berenice with you. And don't forget the jewels." After all three hugged, Berenice began helping them organize their belongings, but just outside the situation changed. By the time they gathered all they could carry, the escorts were gone.

Standing outside with their arms full, Berenice and her parents were dumbfounded. "What happened?" her father asked.

Puzzled by their absence, Berenice replied, "I don't know, I couldn't understand what they were saying. Father, we must go back and find Aristotle."

Ptolemy's camp

In his tent, Ptolemy unrolled a map and intently studied the surrounding area when an officer approached. "May I enter?"

Ptolemy looked up and said, "Ah, Captain Lykos. You returned."

"Yes my King."

"And?"

"We found him, as you ordered."

"Alive?"

Lycos nodded.

"Excellent. Bring him here, with an interpreter. There is one more task, and this is more critical than anything I have ever asked of you."

Lycos motioned to a soldier outside who escorted a man covered in dirt and filth into the tent. Slowly walking into the candlelight, the face of Karpos the prisoner came into view.

Before the interpreter arrived, Lycos took the opportunity to ask a question. "My King...why?"

"Why did I order you to fetch this man?"

"Yes, forgive me, but he has nothing that will help us here."

Now standing directly in front of Karpos and looking into his eyes, Ptolemy slowly said, "Oh, I disagree. Every man can serve a purpose, even one as foul smelling as our friend here."

"Sure, but a prisoner?"

Ptolemy, reflecting on Cleo, whose loyalty was later found to be with Perdiccas, said, "I needed someone familiar with the infrastructure of this area, yet outside his reach. Perdiccas could have men anywhere, especially in the local administrations. Besides, Karpos here has the exact skills we need."

When the interpreter arrived, Ptolemy motioned for all three men to stand around an open map on his table. Looking directly at Karpos, Ptolemy asked through the interpreter. "Do you recognize this area?"

Karpos leaned in and started to run his fingers across the map, following the hand drawn rendition of the Nile's path through the desert. He grunted and mumbled as he tapped the map, and the interpreter did his best to translate. "He does. He said he worked on the levies, here, and here."

Ptolemy grinned. "I was hoping he'd say that." Now looking directly at Karpos, Ptolemy asked, "Do you know who I am?"

Karpos nodded and said proudly, "Ptolemy."

"Tell him the future of Egypt rests on this battle, and I need his help." Karpos took a deep breath and nodded.

Ptolemy then huddled the men in close and continued in a low voice. "I want the two of you to listen very carefully."

Chapter 27

Perdiccas' camp

In the torchlight, Kallisto concluded his report to his perturbed King by adding, "And we cannot forget the food stores. They're also critically low."

Perdiccas scowled while he chugged more wine and swallowed his bread. "Then cut the rations down again. Just tell'em we'll be feasting in the streets of Alexandria soon."

Not wanting to bring the wrath of his King upon him, Kallisto didn't mention that the entire legion was already hungry and angry, so he simply said, "Yes, my King," and left. Passing him in the entryway, General Eumenes, the lead guide, and several of his top men then stepped in and bowed their heads.

Perdiccas was usually pleased to see his most favored General, but had no patience this evening for introductory comments. "I'm tired of these little river games. We will not be sidetracked any further. If you don't cross that river and kill Ptolemy within two days, I'll find someone that can."

Unaffected by the intimidation, General Eumenes stood unmoved. In a calculated manner he replied, "My King, Ptolemy's mistake was to leave the city unprotected. By capturing the city first, we'll have the advantage of supplies and defenses.   And if he returns, I'll personally give you Ptolemy to do with as you please."

"And what if he doesn't return?"

"Then you will have your empire anyway. We can deal with him later, at a time of our choosing."

Perdiccas twisted his neck to the side until it cracked. "Did you not hear me? You have two days."

The guide began to speak when Eumenes silenced him. Carefully choosing his words, Eumenes responded instead, "Our guide has advised us to move further up river before attempting another crossing. The marsh at this part of the river is extremely dangerous."

"Two days," was the only response from Perdiccas, and then with the back of his hand he waved everyone away.

Ptolemy's camp

Meeting at a nearby hill, Ptolemy gave his senior officers a full view of the Nile River and the theater of war below them. Standing on the elevated ground gave them an entirely new perspective of everything. From this viewpoint, the desert expanded endlessly into the distance, while the Nile weaved its green path towards the sea.

Ptolemy began with the brutal reality of their situation. "He outnumbers us by at least four to one. His legion has cavalry, infantry, and war elephants. And, just last night, we confirmed that he has Eumenes with him." Fully knowing what General Eumenes is capable of, a few of the men looked at each other with grief stricken expressions.

Using a stick, Ptolemy then kneeled and etched a line in the dirt following the contours of the river. "His legion is splintered into five groups - primarily located across the river in this area." He then made five Xs in the dirt. "But they're traveling in a closely coordinated fashion, telling me they all move under one command."

One of the officers then made a conclusion. "He's not delegating."

Ptolemy stood and gave an approving nod. "Exactly. And that works in our favor. I think you all know we won't survive another battle alone, not against the full force he brings. We need an ally." Ptolemy then turned around and looked at the Nile. "That river my friends, doesn't just give life."

Ptolemy then brought everyone's attention back to his diagram in the dirt. "I need to know the exact place of his next crossing. No guesses. And I must know this without any doubt."

Knowing their leader expected intelligent input, the officers carefully contemplated the options. Finally, Nikanor kneeled next to Ptolemy and carefully said, "We can not force him, but..." Ptolemy listened carefully as

Nikanor formulated his thought, "...it's possible to draw him to a place of our choosing. If we were camped in the valley behind us, it would be his clear advantage to attack from the surrounding hills."

Another man, Neleos, stepped forward and injected himself, "If I were to engage the enemy there, I would cross up river, in this region." Circling a section of the Nile outlined in the dirt, he explained, "A crossing down river would not be expected. It's almost half a day's walk in the heat of day, but even a large army could quickly span this distance without detection in the night."

Nikanor nodded in agreement. "And more than that, this is the only area where the river banks are low enough to allow a cavalry with elephants to cross." Standing to study the terrain once again, Nikanor confirmed his conclusion, "Yes, to attack us in that valley, he must cross there."

Ptolemy nodded with pride as his men completely aligned their thinking with his. Another stepped forward and added, "Give me twenty men, and by nightfall, I can create the illusion of camps for an entire legion."

After most men voiced agreement, Ptolemy then issued his orders. "Paramonos, I want you to light those campfires. But don't make them obvious. They need to be small, as if you're attempting to hide them. And erect as many tents as you can. Nikanor, set your platoons here as our flanking force. The rest of you, bring your men to this region. Keep all horses back. There must be perfect silence by the river. And I want forward scouts hidden in the banks, from here, to here."

Ptolemy then noticed one in the group stood with doubt in his eyes. "Stephanos, do you have concern to voice?"

Stephanos shook his head and replied, "Whether we face them on this side of the river or theirs, or Alexandria or Memphis, they still outnumber us by at least four to one. We'll be slaughtered where we stand."

Reflecting on the fact that Alexander would have harshly punished anyone making such a statement, Ptolemy tempered his response. "A wise teacher once told me that war is not won by dying in battle." He then put a warm hand on the doubting man's shoulder. "Trust me. We'll be smarter than that."

"Smarter?" Stephanos shrugged off Ptolemy's hand and added, "This is insanity!"

Ptolemy started to reply but stopped himself and turned to the other officers. "Leave us."

Once they were alone, Ptolemy didn't temper his voice any longer. He placed his large frame two inches from Stephanos and said, "Listen!"

But Stephanos took advantage of their friendship and quickly snapped back, "No! Listen to me Ptolemy. Those men love you, yet you so easily send them to their deaths!"

"Stephanos, if that's what you believe, then it's already over and we have lost."

"What I believe doesn't matter. His legion is twenty thousand. Twenty thousand!"

"Enough! I know the numbers."

"Then why Ptolemy? Why do you send what's left of our men to their deaths like this? I cannot participate in such decisions."

Ptolemy rubbed his face and replied, "Stephanos, don't you realize the future of Alexandria is bigger than you and I, and all this? There are no more decisions here but one. And that is, what kind of future do you want?"

Stephanos shook his head. "But those men..."

Ptolemy interjected, "Those men are warriors, and all they need to be victorious, in any mission, is absolute belief in what they do. But if their leader doesn't believe in the destiny of Alexandria, then they won't, and their deaths will surely come. And they will be meaningless. Stephanos, you must be their leader, which means absolute commitment. They can never see doubt in your eyes. Never! If you don't believe in Alexandria, and all it stands for, then speak it now while we're alone."

Stephanos spoke freely. "I know you have plans, but right now, Alexandria is nothing but what you tell us it will be some day. Is that enough to die for?"

"Yes. It is for me. And it is for Perdiccas as well. Stephanos, I love you as I love all the other men that stand with me today. But Alexandria is worth all of our lives."

Stephanos took a deep breath and thought for a moment. His expression changed as he realized all his concerns were dwarfed by the overwhelming conviction of Ptolemy. He looked up with heavy eyes and nodded.

Ptolemy then decided that Stephanos needed something more to inspire his confidence. He put his arm around him and spoke softly to ensure his voice did not carry. "I want you to listen carefully to what I'm about to tell you. You must not utter a word of this to anyone, you understand?"

Stephanos nodded and said, "Not a word, I swear."

"Good. Take another look at the river below us."

Ptolemy continued whispering details of his plan as Stephanos produced a large, devious grin.

Chapter 28

For the second afternoon in a row, as the sun hung low in the desert sky, hundreds of small campfires were being lit next to empty tents. The men in charge of creating the illusion were busy maintaining the fires and moving various objects, ensuring any outside observer would see an active encampment. Just as Ptolemy directed, when viewed from a distance, it appeared as if a small legion inhabited the valley.

From his vantage point just above the river, Ptolemy scanned the dramatic horizon and listened carefully for an attacking force. Although there were no signs of Perdiccas, he could feel an energy building in the dry desert air. He removed the white headdress used to shield his neck and shoulders from the burning afternoon sun, and let the early evening breeze flow through his hair. The glow of the sunset warmly illuminated his dirty face and the bronze plate of armor on his chest. His war helmet and spear, heavily dented and scratched from years of battle, were on the ground by his feet.

Stephanos approached from behind and broke the silence. "He's getting closer. I can feel it."

Without turning to face him, Ptolemy nodded in agreement and then slowly reflected, "He once saved my life you know."

"Perdiccas?"

"Yes." Taking a deep introspective breath, Ptolemy explained, "When Alexander first brought us through Gaza, a battle broke out. It wasn't anything we couldn't handle, but as we pushed forward, a rogue force managed to break through our rear lines. Our infantry was so caught off guard they couldn't even slow'em down. By the time we realized what was happening, it was too late. We tried to surround Alexander to protect him, but they came at us from all directions, drawing each of us away, including me. Alexander was thrown from his horse and that's when these two big Persians were on him. I ran to his side and fought, but instead of saving my King...my friend, I was clubbed to the ground." Ptolemy chuckled, "Some savior I was. I would have been killed but Perdiccas appeared out of nowhere. His sword took their lives before they knew what hit them."

Stephanos questioned, "I don't understand. How can he forsake someone he experienced so much with, just for more territory?"

"Oh make no mistake about it. He doesn't come just for Egypt. He comes for his ego. He comes for me. Whatever happens tonight, by morning, only one of us will be alive." Ptolemy's own words sat in his gut like a rock.

Royal Palace, Alexandria

As Berenice and her parents entered the Royal Palace, they were greeted by an anxious Aristotle, who was clearly expecting them. Wasting no time, he bypassed all pleasantries. "You made the right decision in returning. Given the new parameters before us, I concluded that it's best you're here." Giving her parents a quick nod of respect, Aristotle then added, "Come quickly," as he waddled his large frame into the main hall. "A messenger just arrived with news of Ptolemy."

Berenice stopped walking and held tightly to her fathers arm, bracing herself. Aristotle also stopped, took two deep breaths and gave the grave news. "It's started. He's encountered Perdiccas and suffered great losses defending an Egyptian fortress. But thus far, our enemy has been held."

Without making a sound, Berenice's expression screamed until Aristotle finally noticed. "Oh, my dear. I'm so sorry. And yes, he lives! Ptolemy lives!"

Lowering her head, Berenice wiped tears of relief from her eyes, then swallowed and straightened up. "You said something has changed?"

Aristotle solemnly answered, "It's not good. His army is severely weakened and far outnumbered. The holy priests have issued a directive to all who hold

Ptolemy in their hearts. Tonight is a ceremony, and it begins with a procession of only those who love him."

"What? Why are they giving up on him? You said he lives!"

In a deep, comforting voice, Aristotle replied, "No my dear, it's not what you think. It's not a funeral. This is...well, this is an ancient ritual of a different kind."

Berenice asked, "What kind of ritual?"

"A ritual of invisible and mysterious forces. This, my dear, is Egyptian magic, and we must respect it. Now come, they're waiting for us."

Considering all the servants and personal guards that would 'hold Ptolemy in their hearts', Berenice expected at least one hundred people to be present. But as they made their way towards the temple, the crowds in the street were much larger, and growing in numbers. Soon the masses were so great people were standing shoulder to shoulder as far as the eye could see. Over one hundred thousand citizens of Alexandria answered the call of the priests, and filled all the roads all the way to the temple.

The people in the streets respectfully stepped aside as the entourage of Aristotle, Berenice, Magas, Antigone, and the guards passed. Berenice and Aristotle felt so much adoration from the citizens of Alexandria, tears streamed from their eyes. Never before had they felt such unity with the Egyptian people, nor imagined just how much they cared for their new leader.

The road turned into a simple dirt path, which finally ended at the temple entrance built into the side of a large hill. The crowd of people watched as the ornate doors slowly opened, and three hairless priests in long white linen robes appeared. With hand motions, they escorted Aristotle and Berenice inside, leaving her parents and the personal guards with the rest of the masses outside. Aristotle whispered to Berenice, "We're about to see something no person outside the priesthood has ever witnessed."

Berenice nervously jumped when the doors were slammed shut and sealed behind her, suddenly extinguishing all sunlight. As their eyes adjusted, the only light down the long, rock corridor leading deep into the hillside came from strange glowing glass orbs carried by each of the priests. The scientific mind of Aristotle pondered the source of the dim light, but respecting the secrecy of their rituals, he didn't probe.

Eventually the corridor tightened, forcing the group into a single file line. In a crouched position, they shuffled deeper and deeper into the hill. The corridor then turned into a puzzling maze of left and right turns, hidden openings, and steep drops. And with every terrifying step, panic grew within Berenice. Soon she was hyperventilating so much Aristotle had to tell her to close her eyes and think of other places. This seemed to help, but then the corridor closed in so much, now Aristotle was having troubles. He had to turn sideways to literally force his large frame between the walls. The air became stifling hot, and the sheer panic of being wedged between walls of rock was overpowering.

Berenice and Aristotle could bear no more and pleaded with their escorts to turn back, but to no avail.

They were pushed on for another ten agonizing minutes until finally the walls began to widen. The corridor then spilled into the most sacred of chambers where the remaining eighteen priests were waiting for their exhausted visitors. The two were quickly taken to the back of the room where they could rest and quietly observe.

Aristotle noticed the dim light produced deceiving shadows in multiple dimensions, like dark mysterious figures moving in the background. Three of the priests then stepped forward and began a harmonic chanting that filled the chamber with long, lingering echoes.

Nile River

Ptolemy sharpened his knife with a small stone and looked upward at the black night. He noted there was no moon and a heavy cloud cover, making the sky absent of all light. He thought to himself, if he were to bring twenty thousand men across that river for a surprise attack, tonight would be the night. Only Ptolemy's tall silhouette was visible when men approached and kneeled. One said, "We have a spotting."

Ptolemy quickly lowered the knife. "Stand. Where?"

"On the far hillside, behind the valley where the false camp was set. We saw one man follow the ridge over the camp. He then quickly returned to the river and crossed in a raft."

"Did he know he was observed?"

"No. And something else. We don't believe this was the first time he spied on our camp. He went straight to it."

Ptolemy quickly ordered, "Send notice to all my unit commanders. Tell them ready themselves - it won't be long". He stood tall and looked into the distance, feeling disappointed he didn't have more concrete news. But suddenly Stephanos approached with a Lieutenant and one of his men.

He looked at Ptolemy with an odd satisfaction in his eyes. "He's coming."

"Where?"

"Exactly where we predicted. He took the bait."

"Tell me all you know."

Stephanos turned to the Lieutenant who took the cue to speak. "This man personally saw at least three regiments including a cavalry pass his location up river. Other scouts down river reported a total of ten additional regiments, all converging to the same location. He's bringing his entire legion, and they're preparing to cross right now."

Ptolemy put his helmet on and picked up his spear. "Let's go."

Stephanos escorted his leader to the river's edge, where a small trail appeared. The trail was not natural, but rather created by Ptolemy's men as they already traversed it several times, silently in the night. Ptolemy followed Stephanos on the trail for a few hundred yards, until they came to a small opening in the reeds where five of Ptolemy's senior officers were quietly waiting.

Ptolemy made eye contact with each man and then peered through the reeds across the river. As planned, this was a shallow crossing point with low banks, but the river was still at least five hundred yards wide, making the other side quickly disappear in the darkness.

Ptolemy addressed his officers one last time before battle. He stood proud and strong, but spoke in a low and rough voice from the lack of sleep. "I know Perdiccas. I know his tactics, and I know the anger in his heart. He plans to crush us under his legion. And once we're dead, he'll crush Memphis and Alexandria, and then he'll hunt down and kill all our families to ensure no children grow to oppose him. But after stretching his reach so far, the Persians will rise against him, forever breaking any hope of unity. He MUST be stopped, here and now!"

Ptolemy then turned his head and brushed his hair back. "His plan is to hit that valley with all he's got by morning. And to do that, he must get all his men across that river tonight. But this man has no patience. He'll order all regiments to cross back to back with no gap in between. By the time the first regiment makes it across, at least half his force will still be in the water. Neleos and Stephanos, that's when he's at his weakest, and that's when you attack. The first regiment will be no more than two thousand men, so you'll be even in numbers. But they'll be tired and wet, and unprepared. I want them pushed back in the river, blocking the other regiments still crossing. Keep them bunched up."

Ptolemy then tapped Nikanor on the chest and said, "You hold until needed. Understand?"

Alexandria

Aristotle and Berenice watched in amazement as the priests made sound and light dance across the sacred chamber like a child's dream. In their amazement, they barely noticed that one priest stepped forward, placed two Papyrus reeds on the table, and aggressively tied them into a knot. The reeds were thrown into a vessel of water, covered tightly and set aside. They then doused the entire table with a thick liquid, and began more intense chanting. Aristotle leaned towards Berenice and whispered, "Blood." She looked back at him with horrified eyes.

The priests all began circling the table, dipping their hands in the blood and spreading it across their faces. One approached Aristotle and Berenice, and touched blood to their foreheads as well.

The intensity of the chanting grew until suddenly a flame appeared on the far end of the room, and was flung over the table in a high arc. When it landed, all sound and all light in the chamber extinguished. Aristotle and Berenice instinctively grabbed each other's hands and stood in the absolute blackness.

The only sound was the panicked breathing of Berenice when suddenly Aristotle and Berenice were both seized and forced upon the large stone table. Berenice cried out and Aristotle did his best to fight free, but the priests overwhelmed them. In the pitch black, their hands and feet were bound, holding them flat on their backs, completely helpless. Berenice wept uncontrollably as sounds of the steel grinding on stone could be heard.

Chapter 29

The Nile River

Twenty yards out in the water, in a small reed raft hidden in the darkness, Rami meticulously scanned the riverbank where the senior officers were receiving their final orders. By tying his raft off to a long wooden pole pushed into the river bottom, he managed to hold it against the current of the Nile. Because he was the first to spot Perdiccas just before the Fort of Camels attack, Rami was rewarded with much greater responsibility, and now, at age fifteen, was in charge of all river security.

Sitting in his raft and watching Ptolemy's silhouette in the distance, this young Egyptian dreamed away. He thought of the day he would return home and tell of his adventures in the war to save Egypt, and how he was actually there, fighting, side by side with Ptolemy. But then the vision of his father came to mind. It was the day he left his family to join Ptolemy's army. He could still hear the last mournful words from the aged stonecutter as he turned his back and said, "If you leave, you're no longer my son."

Rami remembered vividly the look in his mother's eyes when that happened. Tears spilled from her face as she said, "Can't you see? We just want you to be part of something important - something that will be honored. The stones you cut with your father will build Alexandria. But if you leave, your life will mean nothing. Nothing!"

Rami listened to his mother, but knew stonecutting was not the issue. She was really just fearful of him joining an army only to be killed. If he could find his destiny in the battle for Egypt, Rami could rise above the status of a laborer, and forever pull his family from obscurity. He gave his mother a hug and then called out one last time, "Father?" But his father never turned around to face his son again.

In the river, Rami's raft shifted, drawing his attention back to the pole that began to loosen in the mud. He stood to push the pole further in when he noticed movement in the direction of his leader. As his eyes slowly focused, the outline of a man became apparent, hiding in the thick of reeds just feet from Ptolemy.

Rami's heart immediately pounded as he realized this was not one of his men. Obeying orders of complete silence, Rami did not yell out, but rather untied the raft and reached for his paddle. But the man in the reeds realized he was seen by Rami, and quickly pushed his raft from the shore and headed down stream at a startling speed.

Rami knew if this man made it to the other side of the river, Perdiccas would be warned and the entire plan would be in jeopardy. Rami's shaking hands finally found the paddle in his raft and plunged it into the water, but his grip failed and the paddle fell loose.

The enemy spy continued paddling in the direction of the river current, putting even greater distance between the two.

Rami gagged as he leaned over and desperately plunged half his body into the water. Finally his right hand nicked the paddle, but it only pushed it further from reach. Meanwhile, he could hear the enemy spy quickly paddling past him.

The sound of Rami's distant splash caught Ptolemy's attention, but with full faith in his security team, he quickly dismissed it and turned back to his officers to say, "There's not much time until morning. Perdiccas will be crossing soon, if not already. Go to your positions and have your men ready. And not a sound!"

Ptolemy then locked his eyes on his men. "This is it. All our training, our experiences, and our paths in life, have coincided to this very place and time. And now, nothing is left but the fire in our hearts and the swords in our hands. Fight like this is the last day of your lives, and make this the day that defines our future...make THIS, the day that lives proudly in your hearts, and the hearts of all men. Now go!"

The inspired officers all went their various ways. Nikanor disappeared into the night as Ptolemy followed Neleos and Stephanos to their waiting platoons. But unknown to them, news of their plan was quickly on its way to Perdiccas. Down river, Rami was paddling as fast as he could towards the enemy spy, but the distance between the two continued growing, and his arms were already growing weak. He brought the paddle back in the raft, and regained his breath. But then panic grew as he realized there was no way to get help, and no way to catch the spy. And even then, he didn't know what to do if he was able to catch him. Rami was small and slim in stature, and not a trained soldier.

Suddenly Rami realized the enemy spy still had to cross the Nile, then traverse on foot back up river to Perdiccas. Without hesitation, Rami quickly pointed his reed raft towards the opposite shore of the Nile and began crossing.

Down river, the spy stopped his paddling to carefully listen. Not hearing a sound from the direction of his pursuer, he assumed a successful evasion and angled his raft to the other side as well. Being a much larger and robust man, he was far from exhausted. The force and speed of his paddling increased, putting him minutes from the other side. And a short run from there would be all that was needed to bring the crucial warning to Perdiccas.

Finally, on the far side of the river, Rami landed in between the reeds of the riverbank, stumbled off his raft and collapsed in the mud. With muscles pushed beyond all limits of fatigue, his back and arms quivered in pain, but after a few breaths he was able to push himself up. Alone and deep in enemy territory, Rami squinted to get a view of the dark terrain when he noticed what appeared to be large mound just above the riverbank. Climbing in that direction, he found himself on elevated ground.

In the distance, something caught Rami's eye. Five hundred yards up river, Rami could see the light of hundreds of small torches moving towards the river and lining the bank. There were also several torches making their way into the water. "They're crossing," he thought to himself.

Turning in the opposite direction, Rami's mind immediately thought of the spy that was trying to warn Perdiccas of Ptolemy's trap. All visions of glory that Rami dreamed of were replaced with shame. It would be his failing that would cost Ptolemy and his army their lives and the entire battle to save Egypt would be over.

Suddenly, Rami heard footsteps sloshing at the water's edge where his raft was stowed. He silently crouched low when the frame of a large man came into view just ten feet away. The man pushed the raft out in the river, and then turned directly towards Rami.

Rami's opportunity for glory finally came. His heart raced, but his mind was laser-focused on a single thought: Kill.

Chapter 30

Perdiccas stood at the edge of the river watching his first regiment enter the water. Leading the regiment were several guides, each holding torches to light their way. Anxious to reach Ptolemy's camp by sunrise, Perdiccas had a change of mind. "Send in another now, down river."

Frustrated, General Eumenes immediately replied, "The water deepens in each direction. This is the only point where they can cross on foot."

Perdiccas angrily snapped back, "I don't care. Just find a way", then turned his back to Eumenes.

On the other side of the river, Ptolemy and Stephanos waited with their men, hidden in the darkness. The two leaders intently studied a light growing across the water. From all the battles they fought together, they both knew very well the brutal violence and death the light brings. Ptolemy lowered his head and thought about Berenice. A vision of her laughing by the shore flashed in his tired head when Stephanos whispered, "Wait. Something's wrong."

"What?"

"The light. It comes from many torches."

"And?"

"Look at the distance it spans." Stephanos swallowed and grimly continued. "This is more than one regiment. He's sending at least one more, maybe a third...we don't have enough men."

Ptolemy replied, "I don't have time to explain. Just know that I have no doubt in you, or our men. Our destiny is much bigger than tonight. All you need to do is trust in me, as I trust in you." Ptolemy looked into the darkness and then back to Stephanos. "I must leave now, but I'll return. You will know what to do." Ptolemy then rushed away into the dark.

By leaving the immediate area himself, Ptolemy was able to retain absolute secrecy in his next task. He quickly navigated his way down a path that winded over a small hill and back down into a valley. At this point, the only visible light came from a small fire at the far end of a clearing. Patiently waiting there was a young man, personally sent by Ptolemy in the previous days.

When Ptolemy approached, he didn't waste any time issuing his orders. "Light'em both."

The young man excitedly sprang to his feet and immediately jolted away. As he ran, he kept repeating the word, "both" in his head. Deep in the hills he finally reached the valley where a false camp was established as bait for Perdiccas. Two men were waiting there when the young man approached completely out of breath.

"Now!"

One man quickly asked, "How many, boy?"

"Both. He said to light them both!!"

The two men looked at each other and nodded. They carefully retrieved arrows from a bag, dipped them into a small campfire and with great precision, launched them into the black night towards two separate hills.

Dried brush that was carefully placed days earlier quickly caught on fire and within minutes, both hilltops were completely ablaze, sending two brilliant sources of light into the dark night.

The growing light from the direction of the false camp caught the spy's attention on the far side of the river. His eyes gazed in the distance and then back down to the river's edge where he found Rami's raft. He didn't understand the light that he saw, but he did know that he had a lot of terrain to cover, and he also knew it was critical he warn Perdiccas before his legion completed its crossing.

Bending down to stretch his legs, the spy prepared for a long distance sprint when a mass of energy suddenly smashed into his side knocking him off his feet and into the river. Next to him in the shallow water was Rami, who quickly rose to his feet. Aware that his small size and frailty was no match for his experienced opponent, Rami immediately attacked again, landing on the spy's head and grabbing his hair. Rami then dug his feet into the muddy bottom and began pulling as quickly as he could out to deeper water. Being an expert swimmer, Rami gambled on the chance that this is where he would have an advantage.

The large man was still stunned by the veracity of Rami's attack and unable to gain his footing. Soon the ground disappeared below Rami's feet, so he started to swim out to deeper water. As the spy came to his senses, he panicked and latched tightly onto Rami's arm.

He then spun around with incredible strength, grabbed Rami's hair and pushed himself above water by pushing Rami's head down. Rami took a deep breath as his head was violently pushed under. But instead of fighting it, Rami conserved his energy, and his air. He extended his arms until he could feel the familiar submerged reeds from the river bottom. Rami and his friends used these when they were children, to see who could hold their breath the longest. With a firm grasp on one, he pulled himself even further under the water until he hit the murky bottom. As he expected, the spy's grip on Rami's hair was released, but Rami didn't release the spy. He grabbed the fabric around the spy's waist and pulled.

Rami could hear muffled screams as his opponent panicked and fought to reach the surface. But Rami never let go, despite his own desperation to breathe. Soon, the struggling and submerged sounds stopped. But by this time, Rami had pushed himself beyond all limits, and consciousness began to fade. In his struggle, Rami let too much air out of his own lungs and lost all buoyancy. His limbs became weak and completely numb. He tried to kick to the surface, but his legs wouldn't move.

When his hands loosened their grip on the spy's body, it gently floated past him. Seeing that, Rami felt a sense of relief, but lack of oxygen made his mind wander. He closed his eyes and pictured his father and mother trying to stop him from leaving. His father's mocking voice rang out in his head, "He wants to fight with Ptolemy - thinks he will be a hero." Then his mother's voice, "He's too young."

Deep in his mental haze, Rami heard a dull, distant splash from a man jumping in the water and frantically reaching down for him, but it was too late. Rami's mouth opened and his chest inhaled, filling his lungs with cold water. His last sensation was that of convulsions as ultimate darkness closed in.

Menes Station Water Dike, the Nile River

Half of a day's walk up the river, standing on a large, man-made structure of dirt and rock, five men also noticed the light, far in the distance. These were the men sent on a secret mission under direct orders from Ptolemy, and known only by Ptolemy. They stood on top of a dike that diverted the river into several directions for irrigation. From their vantage point, they carefully studied the light.

"That's the two," one of them exclaimed.

Captain Lykos turned to Karpos and patted him on the back. "Let's hope our friend from the prison knows what he's doing." Karpos didn't understand the words Lykos spoke, but gleamed with excitement. He motioned to all four men, who in turn began to help Karpos lift the log that he put in place the night before. As it moved, dirt and rock began falling, and soon more came crumbling down. Within minutes, the entire structure buckled, and high-pressure water began spraying through the dirt causing more structure to collapse.

The men ran back to safe ground as river water that was diverted to local farmlands for generations returned to its original flow. They watched in amazement as a wave, several feet high, roared down the Nile.

Alexandria

In the pitch-black chamber, Aristotle and Berenice were completely helpless. Laying face up on the stone table, with arms and legs tightly strapped, all they could do was listen to the priests as they continued their secret ceremony. The sound of a knife being sharpened on stone terrified Berenice to the point of complete panic.

Aristotle tried to put her at ease, but telling her death will be quick didn't help. Suddenly, a large amount of water was poured on their faces, making them choke and gag. Both flung their heads side-to-side, trying to gasp for air.

Eventually the water stopped, and the two were able to calm down and breathe again. But once they did, the sound of the knife being sharpened became more apparent. It rang in Berenice's ear until she finally cried, "STOP!" And this time, the sound stopped. But then footsteps slowly approached, and the eerie sound of the knife now dragging across the table, came closer and closer.

Chapter 31

The Nile River

Waiting for Ptolemy's return, Neleos and Stephanos held their men at bay as the growing light from enemy torches loomed over the water, making the caged energy from Ptolemy's forces grow to unbearable levels. But with several regiments crossing the river side by side, Perdiccas managed to bring an initial five thousand men in the first wave, twice that of Ptolemy's. And directly behind them, was the overwhelming force of fifteen thousand more.

Neleos gritted his teeth and muttered to Stephanos, "I told you this was suicide. Where is he?"

"Doesn't matter. He put his trust in us, so just focus on your job. When they reach dry ground, we hit'em."

Neleos shook his head. "Thousands of lives at stake here. It's all very well that he trusts in us, but should we still trust in him? Are we to die for something that only exists in one man's mind? Alexandria, the lighthouse, the library – all dreams."

Stephanos began to reply when the distant sound of water sloshing and snorting horses finally reached his ears. He knew thousands of men were coming, and battle was just footsteps away. "Neleos, there's no time. We either trust, or we die."

Neleos didn't blink. He finally gave a single nod and said, "For Ptolemy. For the dream. Let's go!"

By the time Ptolemy returned it was too late. Stephanos and Neleos already separated and were discretely issuing their orders down to the lines of men.

The two entire regiments Perdiccas first sent were now on Ptolemy's side of the river stepping onto the riverbank. As the five thousand men trudged out of the water, they quickly assembled into their platoons and started sorting through their weapons. Time was critical. They had to gather themselves and their weapons, and make room for the rest of the legion that was following close behind. Within minutes, the remaining fifteen thousand men would arrive, and once that happened, no opposing force could stop them.

One soldier ringing out his uniform nudged another and said, "We'll surround Ptolemy by sunrise, and be eating his food by noon."

Another soldier then added, "And taking his women by sunset!" The two laughed, and then noticed one of their guides was walking up the river embankment to see the other side. All seemed well until he reached the top, froze mid-step and dropped his torch.

"What's his problem?" the soldier mumbled to his friend.

All of a sudden, the night ignited as two thousand of Ptolemy's men, spanning a distance of a hundred yards, rushed their enemy with a stunning fury.

The guide was instantly stomped to the ground as the men blasted over the ridge and slammed into their enemy.

With armor off and weapons at their feet, most were caught off guard. Their tired sluggish bodies were quickly lofted off their feet, and their exposed bellies pierced by spears and swords. Those still stepping out of the river were hit next, and forced back into deeper water.

The black of night finally started to recede as morning broke. Battle cries and splashing continued as Ptolemy stood on a nearby mound, issuing orders and executing his plan with precision.

But suddenly, everything changed.

The two additional regiments that Perdiccas sent further up river had reached the shore. Ptolemy watched in horror as five thousand additional enemy soldiers surrounded the entire area and closed in. This was twice what he expected, and his men were now far outnumbered.

Ptolemy sharply ordered, "Send in Nikanor. Now!"

A runner then sprinted off, and within minutes, Nikanor's flanking force was on its way. But this was the entirety of Ptolemy's legion. When Nikanor's cavalry arrived, the scene was absolute chaos. Ptolemy's men were now in desperate hand-to-hand combat against an enemy that surrounded them in all directions.

Without hesitation, Nikanor's cavalry burst through the enemy swarm. Swords slashed downward, slicing backs and arms, and crushing skulls, but the valiant effort wasn't enough. The enemy force was still too great, and Ptolemy's men were being slaughtered.

With all his options exercised, the time finally came for the leader to step down and let the fighter from within to emerge. Ptolemy secured his helmet, tightened his grip on his sword, and ran directly into the heart of the battle. He jumped over the river embankment just in time to save one of his men about to be killed. An enemy soldier had his spear raised above a fallen man's chest when Ptolemy arrived and swung his sword with so much power it sliced through both of the soldier's arms, cutting them completely off.

Ptolemy then looked for his next target, and ran towards him and engaged. He fought next to his men just as Alexander taught him, showing nothing but bravery and commitment. And in turn, his men fought harder, just for him.

But in the confusion of battle, one of Ptolemy's men accidentally hit him hard with the back of his sword, causing him to stumble and fall. A larger enemy soldier saw this, and immediately attacked Ptolemy while he was down.

After spotting his leader fighting for his life, Nikanor quickly rode his horse towards Ptolemy's side for protection. Now on his knees, Ptolemy was slashed across the face, with blood spilling from his cheek and ear. He frantically reached for his sword when Nikanor's horse arrived and knocked the enemy attacker to the ground. Ptolemy instinctively dove on his opponent and struck him so hard with his fist it broke facial bones, sending him deep into unconsciousness.

Reaching his hand down, Nikanor helped the severely wounded Ptolemy to the back of his horse and rode to safe ground.

While helping his leader dismount, Nikanor asked, "Where did they come from?"

Ptolemy slid off the horse but didn't answer.

"Hey, you okay?"

Ptolemy looked up with blood covered face and hands, and nodded. He then looked back to the battle to see that Nikanor's force was breaking up the enemy platoons and turning the tide.

"It will be over soon." Nikanor proudly announced.

Out of breath, Ptolemy replied, "No it won't", and then motioned toward the river where in the early morning light, over ten thousand more enemy soldiers were just minutes from reaching the shore.

Nikanor's mouth dropped open in dismay. "This is impossible. We must leave."

Ptolemy weakly replied, "No, keep them there. We must hold them at the river's edge."

Nikanor started to argue when Ptolemy quickly shut him down. "I said, hold them!"

Nikanor finally nodded, and turned his horse back towards the battle. He could see that his men were now aware of the massive force from Perdiccas still crossing the river. He kicked the side of his horse and immediately rushed towards them, barking orders as he arrived to ensure they all stayed fully engaged in the fight.

Out of the battle zone, another muddied man appeared, limping towards Ptolemy. It was Stephanos, and he too was now bloodied and wounded. The two men embraced, and then Ptolemy returned his attention back to the river battle. Stephanos continued looking at his bloodied leader. Even in the face of total devastation, he never saw a man stand with such pride and confidence.

Stephanos then admitted defeat in his own way. "We did our best, didn't we?"

Ptolemy didn't reply.

Stephanos continued. "I'm honored to die by your side my King."

An odd smile appeared on Ptolemy's face, but his gaze never turned from the river.

Stephanos started to turn his eyes back to the river when a knife dropped from Ptolemy's hand and landed in the dirt. Stephanos then noticed that blood was streaming from Ptolemy's face, and dripping down his neck and chest. He grabbed his friend's shoulders and mournfully cried. "Ptolemy?"

Ptolemy slowly slumped to his knees without speaking a word.

Alexandria

Berenice and Aristotle struggled to free themselves in the pitch black, but it was futile. Finally, the approaching sound of the knife stopped right at Berenice's face, causing her to cry out in fear, "No, please no!"

Under Berenice's now deafening screams, Aristotle could hear the sickening sound of flesh being cut. The horrific experience of her torturous death was too much for him, and for the first time in his life, Aristotle's mind began to shut down.

Once Berenice's shrieks died out, it was Aristotle's turn. He felt his arm being grabbed, and again, the sound of cutting began. But through the numbness, he realized it was the thick leather straps being sliced by the blade, and not his arm. Piercing the absolute black, a dim light finally emerged, and there was Berenice, sitting up with the aid of two of the priests. Another helped Aristotle sit up as well.

The two were lifted to their feet where they immediately embraced and cried from their ordeal. After enduring an entire night of ritual magic, the same priests that led them into the chamber the day before, walked them back to the entrance and released them outside to a bright, new morning.

Chapter 32

"Of all evils known, the marsh is home to the most unimaginable."

The words lingered in the minds of all that heard them, haunting them with images of agonizing death. Alternatively, Perdiccas had no interest in the dangers of the river crossing, but rather how soon his army would be on the other side. He paced the shoreline, and walked in and out of his tent several times while cursing under his breath. The boat that was being constructed to carry him across the river was almost ready, and soon he would personally see Ptolemy destroyed, securing Egypt as the major port to his Kingdom. But his men were experiencing slight problems.

Those regiments still crossing at the shallowest part of the river were the first to notice the change. The water became louder, and the pull of the current much stronger. At first the men didn't think much of it, but once the water level started to rise, they knew something was terribly wrong. Soon the water rose several feet and panic set in. Instead of moving forward, platoons of men leaned into the current, struggling to stay in place, but the violent water splashed across their chest and face and they began losing their footing.

Within seconds, the river turned into a raging torrent, ripping hundreds of men at a time off their feet. Frantic cries for help echoed through the desert, but there was nothing that could be done. Soon, entire regiments were pulled away, permanently neutering Perdiccas and his maniacal plans. With a single act of genius, Ptolemy dealt a fatal blow to an entire legion, that just moments before was poised to take all of Egypt.

But the fight was not yet over for those still alive in the river. The look of absolute fear was on every man's face as they fought to keep their heads above water, but enormous swells and splashing forced many to choke and go down. The overwhelming power of the river was relentless, but some managed to shed weapons and clothes, and remain afloat.

The river continued sweeping the survivors downstream until they reached deeper waters where the currents finally slowed. Out of the many thousands of men that drowned, a few hundred survived, and had no choice but to swim for the only shore in sight.

In the distance, they could see a morning mist rising from the marsh.

Despite the nightmare they just experienced, and their ongoing struggle to stay above water, each of the survivors now had a new fear to face. Still echoing in their heads from the previous night was the grave warning from the local guide: "No matter what happens, do not cross down river at the marsh. Of all evils known, the marsh is home to the most unimaginable."

With the river now calming, the typically quiet Egyptian morning returned. Gentle sounds of the river could be heard between occasional coughing and hacking from the men still treading water. A small group of the stronger swimmers were about thirty yards from shore when they decided to stop the splashing and quietly paddle themselves forward. The men nervously scanned the foggy marsh ahead, but there was no sign of danger - just an eerie silence.

They continued sweeping their arms under the water, quietly moving their bodies forward while watching for movement of any kind.

Finally, as they approached the foggy riverbank, ground could be felt under their feet.

The man in front paused, and then nervously laughed as he stood. But then he noticed what looked like a jagged stone floating in the water just feet ahead of him. Through the mist he saw that the stone had two nostrils in front, and two eyes set back. Paralyzed from fear, he couldn't move, but the others around him instinctively pulled back, and that is when the water exploded.

An enormous crocodile launched his body on top of the man, biting down across his shoulder and arm, instantly pulling him under. In shear panic, the men next to him forced their bodies through the now chest-deep water towards land. The crocodile rolled until the man's arm was twisted completely off, then it took another hold onto the man's torso and violently thrust from side to side.

Suddenly another man went down with violent thrashing, and then another. The remaining men could now hear splashing from the marsh as more crocodiles began to fling their bodies into the water.

One of the stronger men locked his eyes on to a long, dark figure that was approaching from shore. The man in front of him screamed out, "What do we do?", as the crocodile closed in. The panicked man in front tried to back up, but the man behind him grabbed his shoulders and pushed him forward, using him as a shield. The crocodile didn't hesitate, and quickly took the man in front down with a fury. The man that pushed him forward took advantage of the opportunity and raced for shore.

Hearing even more cries of death behind him, he knew he had to be stronger and faster to live. Adrenalin pumped through his body as he stepped out of the water, but the ground was boggy and his feet sunk deep into the mud. On his third step, his leg went so far into the muck he couldn't pull it out. He instinctively struggled but the movement pulled him in even further until he was locked, hip deep in mud. Finally he relaxed, and leaned his torso back and let out a hopeless moan. Behind him the screams and thrashing of the other men in the water continued, but a sound closer to shore caught his attention.

"Cyrus," he called out, "Is that you?" But there was no response. He panted nervously and looked side to side. With no other option, he leaned forward as far as he could and dug his fingers into the soft mud. Using all his remaining strength he desperately pulled but his hands just went further into the mud and his body hardly budged. After trying again, there was no movement at all. He was cemented in.

Then, directly behind him came a loud hissing sound, and then the fast patter of reptilian feet. The exhausted man finally succumbed to his situation and relaxed. He simply closed his eyes and waited for death.

Hundreds of other crocodiles along the marsh slithered into the water and headed towards the middle of the river to continue the slaughter. By the afternoon, not one croc in the area had an empty belly.

Of the hundreds of men that entered the marsh that morning, not one survived.

Chapter 33

The crowds on the streets of Alexandria waited all night for Aristotle and Berenice to emerge from the temple. That morning, when the doors finally opened, the two slowly stepped out into the light, covering their eyes from the bright morning sun. The thousands of people surrounding the temple entrance were staring at Aristotle and Berenice with concerned faces.

Exhausted from their experience, Berenice lowered her head and leaned into Aristotle's chest. He patted her on the back as he led her down the street toward the royal palace, where Berenice's parents were waiting. When they arrived, her mother and father both ran to her and gave a long, heartfelt hug.

Berenice's father looked at Aristotle with lost eyes. Aristotle strongly suggested, "Take the palace guards with you, and leave."

"But where?"

"Anywhere, just not Egypt, or Macedonia. Go find a small village on the sea and lose yourselves."

Berenice mumbled "no" several times, and then looked up. A breeze gently moved her hair, exposing a determined expression. "No! Not without him." She then grabbed her mother's hand and went inside. Aristotle looked at Berenice's father to change Berenice's mind, but he only shrugged and said, "It would be easier to change the flow of the Nile my friend."

The Nile River

In the morning light, General Eumenes explained the river crossing disaster to Perdiccas, who was angrily gritting his teeth.

"How many?" Perdiccas asked.

"We estimate just over three thousand."

Perdiccas grinned, "That's not bad. Seventeen thousand is still enough to take Egypt."

General Eumenes was astounded at the extent of Perdiccas' ignorance. "My King, you misunderstand. We only have three thousand men left."

Perdiccas froze, and then started pacing across his tent repeating, "Three, three, three."

"Our supplies have also been lost. We must depart now for your safety." General Eumenes motioned to two of his captains, who stepped forward to either side of their General.

Perdiccas gave a suspicious look at them, and then quickly began to issue new orders. "If any man tries to abandon his post, kill him without exception. Gather my legion by noon, and get me another route to Alexandria."

It was at that moment that General Eumenes and his men knew what had to be done.

A sudden desert wind blew through the tent making the flaps shutter and the candles blow out. The air was fresh and cool, and it howled a mystical tone as it passed through the ancient Egyptian valley, across the Nile, and over the embankment, until it eventually reached a bloodied Ptolemy.

Alone and lying on his back, Ptolemy could hear the battle cries in the distance fading away. He wanted to rejoin them, to die in battle, but in his deep haze he couldn't move.

The wind reminded him of Berenice, and how her long hair danced in the ocean breeze along the beach. He could feel her tiny soft hand in his, and hear her laughter as she playfully pranced in the sand next to him. "Berenice, my love, I'm so sorry", he whispered.

Ptolemy then coughed up blood and closed his eyes when footsteps approached from the direction of the river. He tried again to sit up, but couldn't. Turning his head to the side, a familiar looking figure was suddenly standing next to him. It was a young boy in a clean white uniform, with pristine armor.

The boy chuckled and said, "It will all be over soon." He then laid his sword down, and sat next to Ptolemy.

Ptolemy murmured, "Alexander?"

The boy didn't reply, but instead took a wet cloth and began to wipe the dirt and blood from Ptolemy's face. For the first time in a long time, Ptolemy felt safe, and cared for. He closed his contented eyes.

Menes Station Water Dike, the Nile River

Karpos looked at Captain Lycos as the curious breeze blew his dusty hair back. A great sense of relief came over all the men as they watched the battle dying out in the valley below. Although some of the enemy made it back to shore, most were swept away in the flood created by Karpos.

Lycos readied a horse and asked the interpreter to approach. He explained to Karpos that he fulfilled his mission very well, but there was one last assignment for him, one of honor.

After receiving instructions, Karpos climbed on the horse and waived goodbye to his new friends.

Alexandria

The next day, a vigil in front of Ptolemy's palace grew to over ten thousand people. With solidarity, everyone waited for news of what happened. Although some left Alexandria out of fear, most of its residents stayed to face their fate with Berenice and Aristotle.

Only a few street vendors opened for business, but commerce was conducted with hardly a spoken word. With such an uncertain future and all the stories of Perdiccas, people were terrified.

At this point, Berenice was completely cried out. She couldn't eat and sat for hours completely exhausted. She was reading a poem that Ptolemy wrote her when commotion was heard outside the Palace. Looking out her window, Berenice saw a boy running to the crowd of people. He pointed to the far end of the city where a lone man was approaching on horse. She called out, "Mother, come quick", as she ran from her chamber to join the people outside.

Magas and Aristotle were already there when Berenice ran to their side and quickly asked, "Father, is it him?"

Magas sadly replied, "No my dear, it's not. I'm sorry."

The horse was clearly overheated and stressed from a long run, but it had the dressings a war-horse, instantly indicating this was a message directly from the battle scene. It had difficulty walking, and the man on its back, equally exhausted, struggled just to stay on. As word spread more people filled the streets to hear the fate of Egypt. Soon, there were so many people, the horse couldn't proceed, and the man slumped off and fell to his knees.

Berenice pushed through the crowd and approached the exhausted man. When he looked up, Berenice raised her hand to her mouth in shock. It was Karpos.

He struggled to his feet and took a swallow of water from a vessel handed to him. He looked at the tormented expression on Berenice and everyone else surrounding him. Over one hundred thousand people crowded in the streets, waiting to hear the fate of Ptolemy, and thus the fate of Alexandria and their very lives. They all braced themselves for bad news.

Karpos lowered his head in the enormity of the moment and mumbled to himself. Berenice was terrified when she saw tears begin to drop from his face. But then, with an emotional burst of energy, he stretched out his arms and raised his head exposing a magnificent expression of relief. Drawing a large breath, he shouted with all the energy in his being, "PTOLEMY!!!"

The sound of freedom echoed through the streets, causing a jubilant roar from the crowds. But Berenice didn't react. She refocused back on Karpos, yelling above the crowds, "Is he okay. What of Ptolemy?"

The woman who brought the water attempted to translate. Karpos began talking quickly and then the woman spoke. "He doesn't know. Many men were killed. Something about Ptolemy's plan, and water. I can barely understand him. He doesn't know if Ptolemy lives, but said he is forever indebted to him." Karpos looked around at all the faces in the street as he continued. The woman translated. "All of you are indebted to him. Ptolemy, our King, our savior."

Chapter 34

The Nile River

At the opposite side of the river where Perdiccas camped, General Eumenes now stood in sunlight as a soldier approached.

"General, a small vessel has made several crossings this morning. Men from Ptolemy's army are on their way."

General Eumenes nodded. "How many?"

"Only twenty or so. And horses."

General Eumenes was prepared for this. He already put on a clean uniform and polished his sword. His senior staff did the same and stood behind him as he waited.

The camp that once housed a legion of twenty thousand men under the command of Perdiccas had dwindled down to less than three thousand. The scattered men were starving and weak, and prepared to die.

But just as General Eumenes predicted, this small envoy was not an act of aggression. One of the horses separated and ran directly to Eumenes and stopped. The dust from the horse's hooves blew away in the strong desert wind. The rider had bloodstained fabric wrapped around his head and face, with part of the wrappings flapping in the breeze. The morning sun was brighter than it had been for days.

The rider dismounted slowly with significant discomfort and approached General Eumenes. He then removed the wrapping across his face.

A stunned voice from the group said, "General Ptolemy."

Eumenes and his men all kneeled and bowed their heads with respect. General Eumenes then reached out his hands and presented his sword to Ptolemy, which was quickly accepted.

Ptolemy motioned for General Eumenes to rise, and then issued his demand with a single word: "Perdiccas."

General Eumenes pointed to a large tent. "There."

Ptolemy thought this could be a last desperate trap set by Perdiccas, and cautiously approached. At the entrance, he gripped the sword tightly, and then flung the leather flap open.

Inside, things were in complete disarray. As his eyes adjusted, Ptolemy then saw Perdiccas dead on the ground with stab wounds to his chest and back. Knowing he was out of sight from the others, Ptolemy grabbed his belly and winced in pain from his battle wounds, but then quickly straightened up.

His attention turned to a table in the center of the room, and the two items carefully placed there for Ptolemy to see: Alexander's legendary ring, symbolizing his rule over the largest empire ever amassed, and a very old, but familiar looking parchment.

Outside, General Eumenes watched in awe as the remainder of his army came out of their tents and ran towards Ptolemy's envoy. Large containers were being opened and bread was being handed out to his men.

"I don't believe this," General Eumenes thought to himself. "He brought food for his enemy."

Suddenly Ptolemy came out of the tent and mounted his horse. General Eumenes swung around just in time to watch him ride off towards another of his platoons that crossed earlier that morning. Eumenes realized that after many years of brutal fighting and death, war was finally over.

Ptolemy rode to his soldiers by the river, but before he could dismount, they said there was something he needed to see. Two men then escorted Ptolemy on horseback much further down river, where a third man was sitting on a mound just above the embankment.

Ptolemy climbed off his horse and walked up to the man. It was one of the Egyptians providing river security the night before. The Egyptian sat with a somber expression on his face, and hardly looked up. The interpreter stepped up and told him to repeat for Ptolemy what he told the others earlier that morning. The Egyptian nodded and slowly began speaking. The interpreter followed, "He said it was last night, before the fighting started. He saw a spy scouting the locations of our platoons. He tracked him, but lost him in the dark. He said he came to this side of the river to try and find the spy before he reached Perdiccas, but failed." The Egyptian lowered his head in shame, and then continued. "He said that he was just over there when he heard it." The Egyptian pointed to the river, to a bank with heavy brush and reeds. "There was a loud splash. He pushed his raft ashore and came as fast as he could. He saw Rami's raft floating, and then he saw Rami, struggling in the water with the spy." The Egyptian shook his head and looked directly at Ptolemy. "He said Rami was just a boy. He tried to save him." The Egyptian motioned to the lifeless body of the young Egyptian. "He tried. He keeps repeating, he tried, he tried."

Ptolemy placed his hand warmly on the man's shoulder, and then kneeled next to Rami's body. "I want it prepared and returned to Alexandria. Find his father and mother and bring them to the city as well. He will be honored with the others, and all will know his sacrifice was not that of a boy, or just a man, but that of a true hero."

As the soldiers back at Perdiccas' camp ate the food that Ptolemy provided, they felt an overwhelming sense of relief. For the first time since the campaign started, laughter could even be heard.

General Eumenes watched with delight as his men ate with Ptolemy's, but then the wind blew the leather flaps on the royal tent so hard it caught his attention. He went inside where they previously killed Perdiccas and to his astonishment, Alexander's ring was still on the table and only the parchment was taken.

Looking at his General, one of the men declared, "He forgot the ring."

General Eumenes shook his head. "No, he didn't forget anything."

"Where do we go now?"

Contemplating all the great leaders he has known in his military career, General Eumenes never felt such respect for one man before, as he did at that moment for Ptolemy. "With him. Go with him."

Chapter 35

Sunrise at Alexandria

One bright magical morning, in an ancient land of wonder called Alexandria, a mystical wind from the cosmos blanketed its citizens with new dreams of peace and freedom. In her chamber, a young woman was awakened from those dreams and quickly escorted to the edge of the city where she was shown a mass of approaching soldiers in the distance. Winding their way through the sandy hills and valleys of the Egyptian landscape, the men were returning home from a victorious battle to secure Alexandria's future.

The young woman turned her wet eyes to her parents, and then to her old and wise friend who never left her side. Her expression begged for permission - permission to believe. They all warmly looked back at her, nodding their heads in approval. Her eyes flooded with tears as she cried with overwhelming joy.

In the distance, a lone horse separated from the mass of soldiers and raced towards the city. The rider was tall and blond, and rode with so much passion and desire even the Gods were moved.

Stroking his long white beard, the wise man pondered all the battles, all the brutality, and all the lives sacrificed just for this beautiful moment. More than just growing pains of a new age, he realized these events were really settlements of debt. Like great inequities in the world, they had to harmonize before mankind could mature and be worthy of a gift as miraculous and advanced as Alexandria.

Excited about his realization, the wise man turned to tell the young woman but she was already gone, running down the hill towards the man she loved.

"Look at that," he whispered to himself in amazement. "This is where the dream begins."

The wise man watched as the last of the stones of Macedonia were helplessly pulled across the desert expanse and into each other's arms. As they embraced, a flash of energy ignited that shined so bright, it became a beacon of inspiration through all ages, for all humanity to see.

*   *   *

The old sleeping man made more anguished sounds and then yelled out, "Stop!" He turned to his side and continued snoring while the little boy looked back to his mother with concern.

The woman put a warm hand on her boy's cheek and then answered his question about the dreams.

"No my dear. They don't sound good."

"So they're bad dreams mommy?"

"Mmmm, I wouldn't say that either. They're just dreams my sweetie, just dreams."

Historical Note

Born in Macedonia, 367 B.C., Ptolemy I, the childhood friend of Alexander the Great and subsequent General in Alexander's legion, was a wise, compassionate but shrewd leader whose astonishing impact on the world is embarrassingly understated in the collective memory of modern civilization.

If Ptolemy's library had survived until present day, and the great artistic and scientific think-tank called Alexandria continued to flourish, attracting the most brilliant of minds from around the world to learn and share according to Ptolemy's vision, human advancement could have far exceeded all imagination. I'm convinced that miracles like space travel, quantum physics, and even manipulation of time would now be child's play.

After the battle with Perdiccas, Ptolemy and Berenice lived a full and wondrous life in Alexandria. Ptolemy continued to ensure the security of Egypt, and used his hard earned freedom to advance his people to amazing heights. And to show their love for the man they called Soter (Savior), the people of Egypt welcomed him as their Pharaoh, turning his vision of a futuristic cosmopolitan city into reality.

Most details and dialogue in this story were the creation of the author; however, the major events and key characters were based on historical facts. And for that reason, much appreciation is given to our honored scholars and historians who have dedicated their lives to piecing together the grand puzzle of our past, enabling a rebirth of insight and storytelling.

For more information about this story or the author, visit at www.mpsoldo.com.